Praise for the Patr

'Clearly one of the major achievements of contemporary British fiction. Stingingly well-written and exhilaratingly funny'   David Sexton, *Evening Standard*

'From the very first lines I was completely hooked . . . By turns witty, moving and an intense social comedy, I wept at the end but wouldn't dream of giving away the totally unexpected reason'   Antonia Fraser, *Sunday Telegraph*

'Wonderful caustic wit . . . Perhaps the very sprightliness of the prose – its lapidary concision and moral certitude – represents the cure for which the characters yearn. So much good writing is in itself a form of health'
Edmund White, *Guardian*

'The Patrick Melrose novels can be read as the navigational charts of a mariner desperate not to end up in the wretched harbor from which he embarked on a voyage that has led in and out of heroin addiction, alcoholism, marital infidelity and a range of behaviors for which the term "self-destructive" is the mildest of euphemisms. Some of the most perceptive, elegantly written and hilarious novels of our era . . . Remarkable'   Francine Prose, *New York Times*

'Perhaps the most brilliant English novelist of his generation'
Alan Hollinghurst

'Beautifully written, excruciatingly funny and also very tragic'
Mariella Frostrup, *Sky Magazine*

'The main joy of a St Aubyn novel is the exquisite clarity of his prose, the almost uncanny sense he gives that, in language as in mathematical formulae, precision and beauty invariably point to truth . . . Characters in St Aubyn novels are hyper-articulate, and the witty dialogue is here, as ever, one of the chief joys' Suzi Feay, *Financial Times*

'Humor, pathos, razor-sharp judgement, pain, joy and every-thing in between. The Melrose novels are a masterwork for the twenty-first century, by one of our greatest prose stylists' Alice Sebold

'Edward St Aubyn, like Proust, has created a world in which no one in their right mind would like to live but which feels real and vivid and hilariously and dangerously vacuous. Who better than he to turn to if your faith in the future of literary fiction is wavering?' Alan Taylor, *Herald*

'The act of investigative self-repair has all along been the underlying project of these extraordinary novels. It is the source of their urgent emotional intensity, and the determin-ing principle of their construction. For all their brilliant social satire, they are closer to the tight, ritualistic poetic drama of another era than the expansive comic fiction of our own . . . A terrifying, spectacularly entertaining saga' James Lasdun, *Guardian*

'The wit of Wilde, the lightness of Wodehouse and the waspishness of Waugh. A joy' Zadie Smith, *Harpers*

'A masterpiece. Edward St Aubyn is a writer of immense gifts' Patrick McGrath

'Irony courses through these pages like adrenaline . . . Patrick's intelligence processes his predicaments into elegant, lucid, dispassionate, near-aphoristic formulations . . . Brimming with witty flair, sardonic perceptiveness and literary finesse'
Peter Kemp, *Sunday Times*

'His prose has an easy charm that masks a ferocious, searching intellect. As a sketcher of character, his wit – whether turned against pointless members of the aristocracy or hopeless crack dealers – is ticklingly wicked. As an analyser of broken minds and tired hearts he is as energetic, careful and creative as the perfect shrink. And when it comes to spinning a good yarn, whether over the grand scale or within a single page of anecdote, he has a natural talent for keeping you on the edge of your seat'   Melissa Katsoulis, *The Times*

'In the end, it is language that provides Patrick – and St Aubyn – with consolation . . . St Aubyn's Melrose novels now deserve to be thought of as an important roman-fleuve'
Henry Hitchings, *Times Literary Supplement*

'Blackly comic, superbly written fiction . . . His style is crisp and light; his similes exhilarating in their accuracy . . . St Aubyn writes with luminous tenderness of Patrick's love for his sons'   Caroline Moore, *Sunday Telegraph*

'St Aubyn conveys the chaos of emotion, the confusion of heightened sensation, and the daunting contradictions of intellectual endeavour with a force and subtlety that have an exhilarating, almost therapeutic effect'
Francis Wyndham, *New York Review of Books*

'The darkest possible comedy about the cruelty of the old to the young, vicious and excruciatingly honest. It opened my eyes to a whole realm of experience I have never seen written about. That's the mark of a masterpiece'   *The Times*

'Edward St Aubyn has transformed his appalling childhood into something dazzling and disturbing. A brilliant satire'
Psychologies Magazine

'St Aubyn is a genuinely creative writer rather than a peddler of misery memoirs and so his elegant, sardonic and often very funny books transcend whatever circumstances led to their making . . . His prose is a pleasure to read and his insights can be as telling as they're funny. And forgiving, too'
Irish Independent

'I've loved Edward St Aubyn's Patrick Melrose novels. Read them all, now'   David Nicholls

'A humane meditation on lives blighted by the sins of the previous generation. St Aubyn remains among the cream of British novelists'   *Sunday Times*

'The sharpest and best series since Anthony Powell's *A Dance to the Music of Time*. St Aubyn dances on the thin ice of modern upper-class manners, the pain of displaced emotions and the hope of happiness'   *Saga Magazine*

'St Aubyn puts an entire family under a microscope, laying bare all its painful, unavoidable complexities. At once epic and intimate, appalling and comic, the novels are masterpieces, each and every one'   Maggie O'Farrell

NEVER MIND

EDWARD ST AUBYN was born in London in 1960.
His superbly acclaimed Patrick Melrose novels are
Never Mind, Bad News, Some Hope (previously
published collectively as the *Some Hope* trilogy),
Mother's Milk (shortlisted for the Man Booker Prize
2006) and *At Last*. He is also the author of the
novels *A Clue to the Exit* and *On the Edge*.

Also by Edward St Aubyn

The Patrick Melrose novels

BAD NEWS

SOME HOPE

MOTHER'S MILK

AT LAST

ON THE EDGE

A CLUE TO THE EXIT

Edward St Aubyn

NEVER MIND

PICADOR

First published 1992 by William Heinemann

First published in paperback 1998 as part of
The Patrick Melrose Trilogy by Vintage

First published by Picador in paperback 2007 as part of
Some Hope: A Trilogy

This edition published 2012 by Picador
an imprint of Pan Macmillan, a division of Macmillan Publishers Limited
Pan Macmillan, 20 New Wharf Road, London N1 9RR
Basingstoke and Oxford
Associated companies throughout the world
www.panmacmillan.com

ISBN 978-1-4472-2747-2

Copyright © Edward St Aubyn 1992, 1998

The right of Edward St Aubyn to be identified as the
author of this work has been asserted by him in accordance
with the Copyright, Designs and Patents Act 1988.

All rights reserved. No part of this publication may be
reproduced, stored in or introduced into a retrieval system, or
transmitted, in any form, or by any means (electronic, mechanical,
photocopying, recording or otherwise) without the prior written
permission of the publisher. Any person who does any unauthorized
act in relation to this publication may be liable to criminal
prosecution and civil claims for damages.

1 3 5 7 9 8 6 4 2

A CIP catalogue record for this book is available from
the British Library.

Typeset by Intype Libra Ltd
Printed and bound by CPI Group (UK) Ltd, Croydon, CR0 4YY

This book is sold subject to the condition that it shall not,
by way of trade or otherwise, be lent, re-sold, hired out,
or otherwise circulated without the publisher's prior consent
in any form of binding or cover other than that in which
it is published and without a similar condition including this
condition being imposed on the subsequent purchaser.

Visit **www.picador.com** to read more about all our books
and to buy them. You will also find features, author interviews and
news of any author events, and you can sign up for e-newsletters
so that you're always first to hear about our new releases.

For Ana

NEVER MIND

1

1

At half-past seven in the morning, carrying the laundry she had ironed the night before, Yvette came down the drive on her way to the house. Her sandal made a faint slapping sound as she clenched her toes to prevent it from falling off, and its broken strap made her walk unsteadily over the stony, rutted ground. Over the wall, below the line of cypresses that ran along the edge of the drive, she saw the doctor standing in the garden.

In his blue dressing gown, and already wearing dark glasses although it was still too early for the September sun to have risen above the limestone mountain, he directed a heavy stream of water from the hose he held in his left hand onto the column of ants moving busily through the gravel at his feet. His technique was well established: he would let the survivors struggle over the wet stones, and regain their dignity for a while, before bringing the thundering water down on them again. With his free hand he removed a cigar from his mouth, its smoke drifting up through the brown and grey curls that covered the jutting bones of his forehead. He then narrowed the jet of water with his thumb to batter more effectively an ant on whose death he was wholly bent.

Yvette had only to pass the fig tree and she could slip into the house without Dr Melrose knowing she had arrived. His habit, though, was to call her without looking up from the ground just when she thought she was screened by the tree. Yesterday he had talked to her for long enough to exhaust her arms, but not for so long that she might drop the linen. He gauged such things very precisely. He had started by asking her opinion of the mistral, with exaggerated respect for her native knowledge of Provence. By the time he was kind enough to show an interest in her son's job at the shipyard, the pain had spread to her shoulders and started to make sharp forays into her neck. She had been determined to defy him, even when he asked about her husband's back pains and whether they might prevent him from driving the tractor during the harvest. Today he did not call out with the '*Bonjour, chère Yvette*' which inaugurated these solicitous morning chats, and she stooped under the low branches of the fig tree to enter the house.

The chateau, as Yvette called what the Melroses called an old farmhouse, was built on a slope so that the drive was level with the upper floor of the house. A wide flight of steps led down one side of the house to a terrace in front of the drawing room.

Another flight skirted the other side of the house down to a small chapel which was used to hide the dustbins. In winter, water gurgled down the slope through a series of pools, but the gutter which ran beside the fig tree was silent by this time of year, and clogged with squashed and broken figs that stained the ground where they had fallen.

Yvette walked into the high dark room and put down the laundry. She switched on the light and began to divide the towels from the sheets and the sheets from the tablecloths. There were ten tall cupboards piled high with neatly folded linen, none of it now used. Yvette sometimes opened these cupboards to admire this protected collection. Some of the tablecloths had laurel branches and bunches of grapes woven into them in a way that only showed when they were held at certain angles. She would run her finger over the monograms embroidered on the smooth white sheets, and over the coronets encircling the letter 'V' in the corner of the napkins. Her favourite was the unicorn that stood over a ribbon of foreign words on some of the oldest sheets but these too were never used, and Mrs Melrose insisted that Yvette recycle the same poor pile of plain linen from the smaller cupboard by the door.

Eleanor Melrose stormed her way up the shallow steps from the kitchen to the drive. Had she walked more slowly, she might have tottered, stopped, and sat down in despair on the low wall that ran along the side of the steps. She felt defiantly sick in a way she dared not challenge with food and had already aggravated with a cigarette. She had brushed her teeth after vomiting but the bilious taste was still in her mouth. She had brushed her teeth before vomiting as well, never able to utterly crush the optimistic streak in her nature. The mornings had grown cooler since the beginning of September and the air already smelt of autumn, but this hardly mattered to Eleanor who was sweating through the thick layers of powder on her forehead. With each step she pushed her hands against her knees to help her forward, staring down through huge dark glasses at the white canvas shoes on her pale feet, her dark pink raw-silk trousers like hot peppers clinging to her legs.

She imagined vodka poured over ice and all the cubes that had been frosted turning clear and collapsing in the glass and the ice cracking, like a spine in the hands of a confident osteopath. All the sticky, awkward cubes of ice floating together, tinkling, their frost thrown off to the side of the glass, and the vodka cold and unctuous in her mouth.

The drive rose sharply to the left of the steps to a circle of flat ground where her maroon Buick was parked under an umbrella pine. It looked preposterous, stretched out on its white-walled tyres against the terraced vines and olive groves behind it, but to Eleanor her car was like a consulate in a strange city, and she moved towards it with the urgency of a robbed tourist.

Globules of translucent resin were stuck to the Buick's bonnet. One splash of resin with a dead pine needle inside it was glued to the base of the windscreen. She tried to pick it off, but only smeared the windscreen more and made the tips of her fingers sticky. She wanted to get into the car very much, but she went on scratching compulsively at the resin, blackening her fingernails. The reason that Eleanor liked her Buick so much was that David never drove it, or even sat in it. She owned the house and the land, she paid for the servants and the drink, but only this car was really in her possession.

When she had first met David twelve years ago, she had been fascinated by his looks. The expression that

7

men feel entitled to wear when they stare out of a cold English drawing room onto their own land had grown stubborn over five centuries and perfected itself in David's face. It was never quite clear to Eleanor why the English thought it was so distinguished to have done nothing for a long time in the same place, but David left her in no doubt that they did. He was also descended from Charles II through a prostitute. 'I'd keep quiet about that, if I were you,' she had joked when he first told her. Instead of smiling, he had turned his profile towards her in a way she had grown to loathe, thrusting out his underlip and looking as if he were exercising great tolerance by not saying something crushing.

There had been a time when she admired the way that David became a doctor. When he had told his father of his intention, General Melrose had immediately cut off his annuity, preferring to use the money to rear pheasants. Shooting men and animals were the occupations of a gentleman, tending their wounds the business of middle-class quacks. That was the General's view, and he was able to enjoy more shooting as a consequence of holding it. General Melrose did not find it difficult to treat his son coldly. The first time he had taken an interest in him was when David left Eton, and his father asked him what he wanted to do. David stammered, 'I'm afraid I don't know, sir,' not daring to admit that he wanted to compose music. It had not escaped the General's attention that his son fooled about on the piano, and he rightly judged that a career in the army would put a curb on this effeminate impulse. 'Better join the army,' he said, offering his son a cigar with awkward camaraderie.

And yet, to Eleanor, David had seemed so different from the tribe of minor English snobs and distant cousins who hung around, ready for an emergency, or for a weekend, full of memories that were not even their own, memories of the way their grandfathers had lived, which was not in fact how their grandfathers had lived. When she had met David, she thought that he was the first person who really understood her. Now he was the last person she would go to for under-standing. It was hard to explain this change and she tried to resist the temptation of thinking that he had been waiting all along for her money to subsidize his fantasies of how he deserved to live. Perhaps, on the contrary, it was her money that had cheapened him. He had stopped his medical practice soon after their mar-riage. At the beginning, there had been talk of using some of her money to start a home for alcoholics. In a sense they had succeeded.

The thought of running into David struck Eleanor again. She tore herself away from the pine resin on the windscreen, clambered into the car and drove the unwieldy Buick past the steps and along the dusty drive, only stopping when she was halfway down the hill. She was on her way over to Victor Eisen's so she could make an early start for the airport with Anne, but first she had to straighten herself out. Folded in a cushion under the driver's seat was a half-bottle of Bisquit brandy. In her bag she had the yellow pills for keeping her alert and the white ones for taking away the dread and panic that alertness brought with it. With the long drive ahead of her she took four instead of two of the yellow pills and then, worrying that the double dose might make her jumpy, she took two of the white ones, and drank about half the bottle of brandy to help the pills down. At first she shuddered violently, and then before it even reached her bloodstream, she felt the sharp click of alcohol, filling her with gratitude and warmth.

She subsided into the seat on which she had only been perched, recognizing herself in the mirror for the first time that day. She settled into her body, like a sleepwalker who climbs back into bed after a dangerous expedition. Silent through the sealed windows, she saw black and white magpies burst from the vines, and the needles of the pine trees standing out sharply against the pale sky, swept clean by two days of strong wind. She started the engine again and drove off, steering vaguely along the steep and narrow lanes.

David Melrose, tired of drowning ants, abandoned watering the garden. As soon as the sport lost a narrow focus, it filled him with despair. There was always another nest, another terrace of nests. He pronounced ants 'aunts', and it added zest to his murderous pursuits if he bore in mind his mother's seven haughty sisters, high-minded and selfish women to whom he had displayed his talent on the piano when he was a child.

David dropped the hose on the gravel path, thinking how useless to him Eleanor had become. She had been rigid with terror for too long. It was like trying to palpate a patient's swollen liver when one had already proved that it hurt. She could only be persuaded to relax so often.

He remembered an evening twelve years before, when he had asked her to dinner at his flat. How trusting she was in those days! They had already slept together, but Eleanor still treated him shyly. She wore a rather shapeless white dress with large black polka dots. She was twenty-eight but seemed younger because of the simple cut of her lank blonde hair. He found her pretty in a bewildered, washed-out way, but it was her restlessness that aroused him, the quiet exasperation of a woman who longs to throw herself into something significant, but cannot find what it is.

He had cooked a Moroccan dish of pigeon stuffed with almonds. He served it to her on a bed of saffron rice and then drew back the plate. 'Will you do something for me?' he asked.

'Of course,' she said. 'What?'

He put the plate on the floor behind her chair and said, 'Would you eat your food without using a knife and fork, or your hands, just eat it off the plate?'

'Like a dog, you mean?' she asked.

'Like a girl pretending to be a dog.'

'But why?'

'Because I want you to.'

He enjoyed the risk he was taking. She might have said no and left. If she stayed and did what he wanted, he would capture her. The odd thing was that neither of them thought of laughing.

A submission, even an absurd one, was a real temptation to Eleanor. She would be sacrificing things she did not want to believe in – table manners, dignity, pride – for something she did want to believe in: the spirit of sacrifice. The emptiness of the gesture, the fact that it did not help anybody, made it seem more pure at the time. She knelt down on all fours on the threadbare Persian rug, her hands flattened either side of the plate. Her elbows jutted out as she lowered herself and picked up a piece of pigeon between her teeth. She felt the strain at the base of her spine.

She sat back, her hands resting on her knees, and chewed quietly. The pigeon tasted strange. She looked up a little and saw David's shoes, one pointing towards her along the floor, the other dangling close to her in the air. She looked no higher than the knees of his crossed legs, but bowed down again, eating more eagerly this time, rooting about in the mound of rice to catch an almond with her lips and shaking her head gently to loosen some pigeon from the bone. When she looked up at him at last, one of her cheeks was glazed with gravy and some grains of the yellow rice were stuck to her mouth and nose. All the bewilderment was gone from her face.

For a few moments David had adored her for doing what he had asked. He extended his foot and ran the edge of his shoe gently along her cheek. He was completely captivated by the trust she showed him, but he did not know what to do with it, since it had already achieved its purpose, which was to demonstrate that he could elicit her submission.

The next day he told Nicholas Pratt what had happened. It was one of those days when he made his secretary say that he was busy, and sat drinking in his club, beyond the reach of fevered children and women who pretended their hangovers were migraines. He liked to drink under the blue and gold ceiling of the morning room, where there was always a ripple left by the passage of important men. Dull, dissolute, and obscure members felt buoyed up by this atmosphere of power, as little dinghies bob up and down on their moorings when a big yacht sails out of the harbour they have shared.

'Why did you make her do it?' asked Nicholas, hovering between mischief and aversion.

'Her conversation is so limited, don't you find?' said David.

Nicholas did not respond. He felt that he was being forced to conspire, just as Eleanor had been forced to eat.

'Did she make better conversation from the floor?' he asked.

'I'm not a magician,' said David, 'I couldn't make her amusing, but I did at least keep her quiet. I was dread-ing having another talk about the agonies of being rich. I know so little about them, and she knows so little about anything else.'

Nicholas chuckled and David showed his teeth. Whatever one felt about David wasting his talents, thought Nicholas, he had never been any good at smiling.

David walked up the right side of the double staircase that led from the garden to the terrace. Although he was now sixty, his hair was still thick and a little wild. His face was astonishingly handsome. Its faultlessness was its only flaw; it was the blueprint of a face and had an uninhabited feeling to it, as if no trace of how its owner had lived could modify the perfection of the lines. People who knew David well watched for signs of decay, but his mask grew more noble each year. Behind his dark glasses, however rigidly he held his neck, his eyes flickered unobserved, assessing the weaknesses in people. Diagnosis had been his most intoxicating skill as a doctor and after exhibiting it he had often lost interest in his patients, unless something about their suffering intrigued him. Without his dark glasses, he wore an inattentive expression, until he spotted another person's vulnerability. Then the look in his eyes hardened like a flexed muscle.

He paused at the top of the stairs. His cigar had gone out and he flung it over the wall into the vines below. Opposite him, the ivy that covered the south side of the house was already streaked with red. He admired the colour. It was a gesture of defiance towards decay, like a man spitting in the face of his torturer. He had seen Eleanor hurrying away early in her ridiculous car. He had even seen Yvette trying to steal into the house without drawing attention to herself. Who could blame them?

He knew that his unkindness to Eleanor was effective only if he alternated it with displays of concern and elaborate apologies for his destructive nature, but he had abandoned these variations because his disappointment in her was boundless. He knew that she could not help him unravel the knot of inarticulacy that he carried inside him. Instead, he could feel it tightening, like a promise of suffocation that shadowed every breath he took.

It was absurd; but all summer long he had been obsessed by the memory of a mute cripple he had seen in Athens airport. This man, trying to sell tiny bags of pistachio nuts by tossing printed advertisements into the laps of waiting passengers, had heaved himself forward, stamping the ground with uncontrollable feet, his head lolling and his eyes rolling upwards. Each time David had looked at the man's mouth twisting silently, like a gasping fish on a river bank, he had felt a kind of vertigo.

David listened to the swishing sound his yellow slippers made as he walked up the last flight of steps to the door that led from the terrace into the drawing room. Yvette had not yet opened the curtains, which saved him the trouble of closing them again. He liked the drawing room to look dim and valuable. A dark red and heavily gilded chair that Eleanor's American grandmother had prised from an old Venetian family on one of her acquisitive sweeps through Europe gleamed against the opposite wall of the room. He enjoyed the scandal connected with its acquisition and, knowing that it ought to be carefully preserved in a museum, he made a point of sitting on it as often as possible. Sometimes, when he was alone, he sat in the Doge's chair, as it was always called, leaning forward on the edge of the seat, his right hand clasping one of the intricately carved arms, striking a pose he remembered from the *Illustrated History of England* he had been given at prep school. The picture portrayed Henry V's superb anger when he was sent a present of tennis balls by the insolent King of France.

David was surrounded by the spoils of Eleanor's matriarchal American family. Drawings by Guardi and Tiepolo, Piazetta and Novelli hung thickly over the walls. An eighteenth-century French screen, crowded with greyish-brown monkeys and pink roses, divided the long room in half. Partially hidden behind it, from where David stood, was a black Chinese cabinet, its top crowded with neat rows of bottles, and its inner shelves filled with their reinforcements. As he poured himself a drink, David thought about his dead father-in-law, Dudley Craig, a charming, drunken Scotsman who had been dismissed by Eleanor's mother, Mary, when he became too expensive to keep.

After Dudley Craig, Mary had married Jean de Valençay, feeling that if she was going to keep a man, he might as well be a duke. Eleanor had been brought up in a string of houses where every object seemed to have been owned by a king or an emperor. The houses were wonderful, but guests left them with relief, conscious that they were not quite good enough, in the duchess's eyes, for the chairs on which they had sat.

David walked towards the tall window at the end of the room. The only one with its curtain open, it gave a view onto the mountain opposite. He often stared at the bare outcrops of lacerated limestone. They looked to him like models of human brains dumped on the dark green mountainside, or at other times, like a single brain, bursting from dozens of incisions. He sat on the sofa beside the window and looked out, trying to work up a primitive sense of awe.

2

Patrick walked towards the well. In his hand he carried a grey plastic sword with a gold handle, and swished it at the pink flowers of the valerian plants that grew out of the terrace wall. When there was a snail on one of the fennel stems, he sliced his sword down the stalk and made it fall off. If he killed a snail he had to stamp on it quickly and then run away, because it went all squishy like blowing your nose. Then he would go back and have a look at the broken brown shell stuck in the soft grey flesh, and would wish he hadn't done it. It wasn't fair to squash the snails after it rained because they came out to play, bathing in the pools under the dripping leaves and stretching out their horns. When he touched their horns they darted back and his hand darted back as well. For snails he was like a grown-up.

One day, when he was not intending to go there, he

had been surprised to find himself next to the well and so he decided that the route he had discovered was a secret short cut. Now he always went that way when he was alone. He walked through a terrace of olive trees where yesterday the wind had made the leaves flick from green to grey and grey to green, like running his fingers back and forth over velvet, making it turn pale and dark again.

He had shown Andrew Bunnill the secret short cut and Andrew said it was longer than the other way, and so he told Andrew he was going to throw him down the well. Andrew was feeble and had started to cry. When Andrew flew back to London, Patrick said he would throw him out of the plane. Blub, blub, blub. Patrick wasn't even on the plane, but he told Andrew he would be hiding under the floor and would saw a circle around his chair. Andrew's nanny said that Patrick was a nasty little boy, and Patrick said it was just because Andrew was so wet.

Patrick's own nanny was dead. A friend of his mother's said she had gone to heaven, but Patrick had been there and knew perfectly well that they had put her in a wooden box and dropped her in a hole. Heaven was the other direction and so the woman was lying, unless it was like sending a parcel. His mother cried a lot when nanny was put in the box, she said it was because of her own nanny. That was stupid, because her own nanny was still alive and in fact they had to go and visit her on the train, and it was the most boring thing ever. She had horrible cake with only a tiny bit of jam in the middle and millions of miles of fluff on either side. She always said, 'I know you like this,' which was a lie, because he had told her he didn't the last time. It was called sponge cake and so he had asked was it for having a bath with and his mother's nanny had laughed and laughed and hugged him for ages. It was disgusting because she pressed her cheek next to his and her skin hung down loosely, like that chicken's neck he had seen hanging over the edge of the table in the kitchen.

Why did his mother have to have a nanny anyway? He didn't have one anymore and he was only five. His father said he was a little man now. He remembered going to England when he was three. It was winter and he saw snow for the first time. He could remember standing on the road by a stone bridge and the road was covered in frost and the fields were covered in snow and the sky was shining and the road and the hedges were blazing and he had blue woollen gloves on and his nanny held his hand and they stood still for ages looking at the bridge. He used to think of that often, and the time they were in the back of the car and he had his head in her lap and he looked up at her and she smiled and the sky behind her head was very wide and blue, and he had fallen asleep.

Patrick walked up a steep bank on a path that ran beside a bay tree and emerged next to the well. He was forbidden to play by the well. It was his favourite place to play. Sometimes he climbed onto the rotten cover and jumped up and down, pretending it was a trampoline. Nobody could stop him, nor did they often try. The wood was black where the blistered pink paint had peeled off. It creaked dangerously and made his heart beat faster. He was not strong enough to lift the cover himself, but when it was left open he collected stones and clumps of earth to throw down the shaft. They hit the water with a deep reverberating splash and broke into the blackness.

Patrick raised his sword in triumph as he reached the top of the path. He could see that the cover of the well was pushed back. He started to search about for a good stone, the biggest one he could lift and the roundest he could find. He hunted in the surrounding field and unearthed a reddish stone which he needed both hands to carry. He placed it on the flat surface next to the opening of the well shaft and hoisted himself up until his legs no longer touched the ground and, leaning over as far as he could, looked down at the darkness where he knew the water was hiding. Holding on with his left hand, he pushed the stone over the edge and heard the plunging sound it made and watched the surface break and the disturbed water catch the light of the sky and gleam back at it unreliably. So heavy and black it was more like oil. He shouted down the shaft where the dry bricks turned green and then black. If he leaned over far enough he could hear a damp echo of his own voice.

Patrick decided to climb up the side of the well. His scuffed blue sandals fitted in the gaps between the rocks. He wanted to stand on the ledge beside the open well shaft. He had done it once before, for a dare, when Andrew was staying. Andrew had stood beside the well saying, 'Please don't, Patrick, please come down, *please* don't.' Patrick wasn't scared then, although Andrew was, but now that he was alone he felt dizzy, squatting on the ledge, with his back to the water. He stood up very slowly and as he straightened, he felt the invitation of the emptiness behind him, pulling him backwards. He was convinced that his feet would slip if he moved, and he tried to stop wobbling by clenching his fists and his toes and looking down very seriously at the hard ground around the well. His sword was still resting on the ledge and he wanted to retrieve it in order to make his conquest complete, and so he leaned over carefully, with an enormous effort of will, defying the fear that tried to arrest his limbs, and picked up the sword by its scratched and dented grey blade. Once he got hold of the sword, he bent his knees hesitantly and jumped over the edge, landing on the ground, shouting hooray and making the noise of clashing metal as he slashed about him at imaginary enemies. He whacked a bay leaf with the flat of his sword and then stabbed the air underneath it with a morbid groan, clutching his side at the same time. He liked to imagine an ambushed Roman army about to be smashed to bits by the barbarians, when he arrived, the commander of the special soldiers with purple cloaks, and he was braver than anybody and saved the day from unthinkable defeat.

When he went for a walk in the woods he often thought about Ivanhoe, the hero of one of his favourite comics, who cut down the trees on either side of him as he passed. Patrick had to walk around the pine trees, but he imagined he had the power to carve his own path, striding majestically through the small wood at the end of the terrace on which he stood, felling with a single blow each tree to his right and left. He read things in books and then he thought about them lots. He had read about rainbows in a soppy picture book, but then he had started to see them in the streets in London after it rained, when the petrol from the cars stained the tarmac and the water fanned out in broken purple, blue, and yellow rings.

He didn't feel like going into the wood today and so he decided to jump down all the terraces. It was like flying, but some of the walls were too high and he had to sit on the edge, throw his sword down, and lower himself as far as he could before he dropped. His shoes filled with the dry soil around the vines and he had to take them off twice and hold them upside down to shake out the earth and the pebbles. Nearer the bottom of the valley the terraces became wider and shallower and he could leap over the edge of all the walls. He gathered his breath for the final flight.

Sometimes he managed to jump so far that he felt like Superman practically, and at other times he made himself run faster by thinking about the Alsatian dog that chased him down the beach on that windy day when they had gone to lunch at George's. He had begged his mother to let him go for a walk, because he loved looking at the wind when it exploded the sea, like smashing bottles against rocks. Everyone said not to go too far, but he wanted to be nearer the rocks. There was a sandy path leading to the beach and while he was walking down it a fat, long-haired Alsatian appeared at the top of the hill, barking at him. When he saw it move closer, he started to run, following the twists in the path at first and then jumping straight down the soft slope, faster and faster, until he was taking giant strides, his arms spread out against the wind, rushing down the hill onto the half circle of sand between the rocks, right up to the edge of the highest wave. When he looked up the dog was miles away up on the hill, and he knew it could never catch him because he was so fast. Later he wondered if it had tried.

Patrick arrived panting at the dried-up river bed. He climbed onto a big rock between two clumps of pale green bamboo. When he had taken Andrew there they had played a game that Patrick invented. They both had to stand on the rock and try to push each other off, and on one side they pretended there was a pit full of broken razor blades and on the other there was a tank full of honey. And if you fell to one side you were cut to death in a million places, and on the other you drowned, exhausted by a heavy golden swim. Andrew fell over every time, because he was so utterly wet.

Andrew's father was wet too, in a way. Patrick had

been to Andrew's birthday party in London, and there was a huge box in the middle of the drawing room, full of presents for the other children. They all queued up and took a present out of the box and then ran around comparing what they'd got. Unlike them, Patrick hid his present under an armchair and went back to get another one. When he was leaning over the box, fishing out another shiny package, Andrew's father squatted down next to him and said, 'You've already had one haven't you, Patrick?' – not angrily, but in a voice like he was offering Patrick a sweet. 'It isn't fair on the other children if you take their presents, is it?' Patrick looked at him defiantly and said, 'I haven't got one already,' and Andrew's father just looked all sad and utterly wet and said, 'Very well, Patrick, but I don't want to see you taking another one.' And so Patrick got two presents, but he hated Andrew's father because he wanted more.

Patrick had to play the rock game on his own now, jumping from one side of the rock to another, challenging his sense of balance with wild gestures. When he fell over, he pretended it had not happened, although he knew that was cheating.

Patrick looked doubtfully at the rope François had tied for him to one of the nearby trees so that he could swing over the river bed. He felt thirsty and started to climb back up to the house along the path where the tractor worked its way among the vines. His sword had become a burden and he carried it under his arm resentfully. He had heard his father use a funny expression once. He said to George, 'Give him enough rope and he'll hang himself.' Patrick did not know what that meant at first, but he became convinced, with a flash of terror and shame, that they were talking about the rope that François had tied to the tree. That night he dreamt that the rope had turned into one of the tentacles of an octopus and wrapped itself around his throat. He tried to cut it, but he could not because his sword was only a toy. His mother cried a lot when they found him dangling from the tree.

Even when you were awake it was hard to know what grown-ups meant when they said things. One day he had worked out a way of guessing what they were going to do: no meant no, maybe meant perhaps, yes meant maybe and perhaps meant no, but the system did not work, and he decided that maybe everything meant perhaps.

Tomorrow the terraces would be crowded with grape-pickers filling their buckets with bunches of grapes. Last year François had taken him on the tractor. His hands were very strong and hard like wood.

François was married to Yvette who had gold teeth you could see when she smiled. One day Patrick was going to have all his teeth made of gold, not just two or three. He sometimes sat in the kitchen with Yvette and she let him taste the things she was cooking. She came up to him with spoons full of tomato and meat and soup and said, '*Ça te plait?*' And he could see her gold teeth when he nodded. Last year François told him to sit in the corner of the trailer next to two big barrels of grapes. Sometimes when the road was rough and steep he turned around and said, '*Ça va?*' And Patrick shouted back, '*Oui, merci,*' over the noise of the engine and the bumping and squealing of the trailer and the brakes. When they got to the place where the wine was made, Patrick was very excited. It was dark and cool in there, the floor was hosed with water, and there was a sharp smell of juice turning into wine. The room was vast and François took him up a ladder to a high ramp that ran above the wine press and all of the vats. The ramp was made of metal with holes in it and it was a funny feeling being so high up with holes under his feet.

When they got to the wine press Patrick looked down and saw two steel rollers turning in opposite directions with no space in between them. Stained with grape juice, they pressed against each other, spinning loudly. The lower railing of the ramp only came up to Patrick's chin and he felt very close to the wine press. And looking at it, he felt that his eyes were like the grapes, made of the same soft translucent jelly and that they might fall out of his head and get crushed between the two rollers.

As Patrick approached the house, climbing as usual the right-hand flight of the double staircase because it was luckier, he turned into the garden to see if he could find the frog that lived in the fig tree. Seeing the tree frog was very lucky indeed. Its bright green skin was even smoother against the smooth grey skin of the fig tree, and it was hard to find it among the fig leaves which were almost the same colour as itself. In fact, Patrick had only seen the tree frog twice, but he had stood still for ages staring at its sharp skeleton and bulging eyes, like the beads on his mother's yellow necklace, and at the suckers on its front feet that held it motionless against the trunk and, above all, at the swelling sides which enlivened a body as delicate as jewellery, but greedier for breath. The second time he saw the frog, Patrick stretched out his hand and carefully touched its head with the tip of his index finger, and it did not move and he felt that it trusted him.

The frog was not there today and so he climbed

wearily up the last flight of steps, pushing against his knees with his hands. He walked around the house to the kitchen entrance and reached up to open the squealing door. He had expected to find Yvette in the kitchen, but she was not there. Bottles of white wine and champagne jostled and clinked as he opened the refrigerator door. He turned back into the larder, where he found two warm bottles of chocolate milk in the corner of the lower shelf. After several attempts he opened one and drank the soothing liquid straight from the bottle, something Yvette had told him not to do. Immediately after drinking he felt violently sad and sat for several minutes on the kitchen counter staring down at his dangling shoes.

He could hear the piano music, muted by distance and closed doors, but he did not pay any attention to it, until he recognized the tune his father had composed for him. He jumped off the counter and ran down the corridor that led to the hall, crossed the hall, and broke into a kind of cantering motion as he entered the drawing room and danced to his father's tune. It was wild music with harsh flurries of high notes superimposed on a rumbling military march. Patrick hopped and skipped between the tables and chairs and around the edge of

the piano, only coming to rest when his father ceased
to play.

'How are you today, Mr Master Man?' asked his
father, staring at him intently.

'All right, thank you,' said Patrick, wondering if it
was a trick question. He was out of breath, but he knew
he must concentrate because he was with his father.
When he had asked what was the most important thing
in the world, his father had said, 'Observe everything.'
Patrick often forgot about this instruction, but in his
father's presence he looked at things carefully, without
being sure what he was looking for. He had watched
his father's eyes behind their dark glasses. They moved
from object to object and person to person, pausing
for a moment on each and seeming to steal something
vital from them, with a quick adhesive glance, like the
flickering of a gecko's tongue. When he was with his
father, Patrick looked at everything seriously, hoping
he looked serious to anyone who might watch his eyes,
as he had watched his father's.

'Come here,' said his father. Patrick stepped closer.
'Shall I pick you up by the ears?'

'No,' shouted Patrick. It was a sort of game they
played. His father reached out and clasped Patrick's
ears between his forefingers and thumbs. Patrick put

his hands around his father's wrists and his father pretended to pick him up by his ears, but Patrick really
took the strain with his arms. His father stood up and
lifted Patrick until their eyes were level.

'Let go with your hands,' he said.

'No,' shouted Patrick.

'Let go and I'll drop you at the same time,' said his
father persuasively.

Patrick released his father's wrists, but his father
continued to pinch his ears. For a moment the whole
weight of his body was supported by his ears. He
quickly caught his father's wrists again.

'Ouch,' he said, 'you said you were going to drop
me. *Please* let go of my ears.'

His father still held him dangling in the air. 'You've
learned something very useful today,' he said. 'Always
think for yourself. Never let other people make important decisions for you.'

'Please let go,' said Patrick. 'Please.' He felt that he
was going to cry, but he pushed back his sense of
desperation. His arms were exhausted, but if he relaxed
them he felt as if his ears were going to be torn off,
like the gold foil from a pot of cream, just ripped off
the side of his head.

'You *said*,' he yelled, 'you said.'

His father dropped him. 'Don't whimper,' he said in a bored voice, 'it's very unattractive.' He sat down at the piano and started playing the march again, but Patrick did not dance.

He ran from the room, through the hall, out of the kitchen, over the terrace, along the olive grove and into the pine wood. He found the thorn bush, ducked underneath it, and slid down a small slope into his most secret hiding place. Under a canopy of bushes, wedged up against a pine tree which was surrounded by thickets on every side, he sat down and tried to stop the sobs, like hiccups, that snarled his throat.

Nobody can find me here, he thought. He could not control the spasms that caught his breath as he tried to inhale. It was like being caught in sweaters, when he plunged his head in and couldn't find the neck of the sweater and he tried to get out through the arm and it all got twisted and he thought he would never get out and he couldn't breathe.

Why did his father do that? Nobody should do that to anybody else, he thought, nobody should do that to anybody else.

In winter when there was ice on the puddles, you could see the bubbles trapped underneath and the air couldn't breathe: it had been ducked by the ice and held under, and he hated that because it was so unfair and so he always smashed the ice to let the air go free.

Nobody can find me here, he thought. And then he thought, what if nobody can find me here?

3

Victor was still asleep in his room downstairs and Anne wanted him to stay asleep. After less than a year together they now slept in separate rooms because Victor's snoring, and nothing else about him, kept her awake at night. She walked barefoot down the steep and narrow staircase running the tips of her fingers along the curve of the whitewashed walls. In the kitchen she removed the whistle from the spout of the chipped enamel kettle, and made coffee as silently as possible.

There was a tired ebullience about Victor's kitchen, with its bright orange plates and watermelon slices grinning facetiously from the tea towels. It was a harbour of cheap gaiety built up by Victor's ex-wife, Elaine, and Victor had been torn between protesting against her bad taste and the fear that it might be in bad taste to protest. After all, did one notice the kitchen things? Did they matter? Wasn't indifference more dignified? He had always admired David Melrose's certainty that beyond good taste lay the confidence to make mistakes because they were one's own. It was at this point that Victor often wavered. Sometimes he opted for a few days, or a few minutes, of assertive impertinence, but he always returned to his careful impersonation of a gentleman; it was all very well to *épater les bourgeois*, but the excitement was double-edged if you were also one of them. Victor knew that he could never acquire David Melrose's conviction that success was somehow vulgar. Though sometimes he was tempted to believe that David's languor and contempt masked regret for his failed life, this simple idea dissolved in David's overbearing presence.

What amazed Anne was that a man as clever as Victor could be caught with such small hooks. Pouring herself some coffee she felt a strange sympathy for Elaine. They had never met, but she had come to understand what had driven Victor's wife to seek refuge in a full set of Snoopy mugs.

When Anne Moore had been sent by the London bureau of the *New York Times* to interview the eminent philosopher Sir Victor Eisen, he had seemed a little old-fashioned. He had just returned from lunch at the Athenaeum, and his felt hat, darkened by rain, lay on the hall table. He pulled his watch out of his waistcoat pocket with what struck Anne as an archaic gesture.

'Ah, exactly on time,' he said. 'I admire punctuality.'

'Oh, good,' she answered, 'a lot of people don't.'

The interview had gone well, so well in fact that later in the afternoon it moved into his bedroom. From that point on Anne had willingly interpreted the almost Edwardian clothes, the pretentious house and the claret-stained anecdotes as part of the camouflage that a Jewish intellectual would have had to take on, along with a knighthood, in order to blend into the landscape of conventional English life.

During the months that followed she lived with Victor in London, ignoring any evidence that made this mild interpretation look optimistic. Those interminable weekends, for instance, which started with briefings on Wednesday night: how many acres, how many centuries, how many servants. Thursday evening was given over to speculation: he hoped, he really hoped, that the Chancellor wouldn't be there this time; could Gerald still be shooting now that he was in a wheelchair? The warnings came on Friday, during the drive down: '*Don't* unpack your own bags in this house.' '*Don't* keep asking people what they do.' '*Don't* ask the butler how he *feels*, as you did last time.' The weekends only ended on Tuesday when the stalks and skins of Saturday and Sunday were pressed again for their last few drops of sour juice.

In London, she met Victor's clever friends but at weekends the people they stayed with were rich and often stupid. Victor was *their* clever friend. He purred appreciatively at their wine and pictures and they started many of their sentences by saying, 'Victor will be able to tell us . . .' She watched them trying to make him say something clever and she watched him straining himself to be more like them, even reiterating the local pieties: wasn't it splendid that Gerald *hadn't* given up shooting? Wasn't Gerald's mother amazing? Bright as a button and still beavering away in the garden at ninety-two. 'She completely wears me out,' he gasped.

If Victor sang for his supper, at least he enjoyed eating it. What was harder to discount was his London house. He had bought the fifteen-year lease on this surprisingly large white stucco house in a Knightsbridge crescent after selling his slightly smaller but freehold house at a less fashionable address. The lease now had only seven years to run. Anne stoutly ascribed this insane transaction to the absent-mindedness for which philosophers are famous.

Only when she had come down here to Lacoste in July and seen Victor's relationship with David had her loyalty begun to wear away. She started to wonder how high a price in wasted time Victor was prepared to pay for social acceptance, and why on earth he wanted to pay it to David.

According to Victor, they had been 'exact contemporaries', a term he used for anyone of vaguely his own age who had not noticed him at school. 'I knew him at Eton' too often meant that he had been ruthlessly mocked by someone. He said of only two other scholars that they were friends of his at school, and he no longer saw either of them. One was the head of a Cambridge college and the other a civil servant who was widely thought to be a spy because his job sounded too dull to exist.

She could picture Victor in those days, an anxious schoolboy whose parents had left Austria after the First World War, settled in Hampstead, and later helped a friend find a house for Freud. Her images of David Melrose had been formed by a mixture of Victor's stories and her American vision of English privilege. She pictured him, a demigod from the big house, opening the batting against the village cricket team, or lounging about in a funny waistcoat he was allowed to wear because he was in Pop, a club Victor never got into. It was hard to take this Pop thing seriously but somehow Victor managed. As far as she could make out it was like being a college football hero, but instead of making out with the cheerleaders, you got to beat young boys for burning your toast.

When she had met David, at the end of the long red carpet unrolled by Victor's stories, she spotted the arrogance but decided that she was just too American to buy into the glamour of David's lost promise and failure. He struck her as a fraud and she had said so to Victor. Victor had been solemn and disapproving, arguing that on the contrary David suffered from the clarity with which he saw his own situation. 'You mean he *knows* he's a pain in the ass?' she had asked.

Anne moved back towards the stairs, warming her hands with a steaming orange mug covered in purple hearts of various sizes. She would have liked to spend the day reading in the hammock that hung between the plane trees in front of the house, but she had agreed to go to the airport with Eleanor. This American Girls' Outing had been imposed on her by Victor's unquenchable desire to be associated with the Melroses. The only

Melrose Anne really liked was Patrick. At five years old he was still capable of a little enthusiasm.

If at first she had been touched by Eleanor's vulnerability, Anne was now exasperated by her drunkenness. Besides, Anne had to guard against her wish to save people, as well as her habit of pointing out their moral deficiencies, especially as she knew that nothing put the English more on edge than a woman having definite opinions, except a woman who went on to defend them. It was as if every time she played the ace of spades, it was beaten by a small trump. Trumps could be pieces of gossip, or insincere remarks, or irrelevant puns, or anything that dispelled the possibility of seriousness. She was tired of the deadly smile on the faces of people whose victory was assured by their silliness.

Having learned this, it had been relatively easy to play along with the tax-exiled English duke, George Watford, who came up from the coast for weekends with the Melroses, wearing shoes that tapered to a quite impossible thinness. His rather wooden face was covered in the thinnest cracks, like the varnish on the Old Masters he had 'shocked the nation' by selling. The English didn't ask much of their dukes in Anne's opinion. All they had to do was hang on to their possessions, at least the very well-known ones, and then they got to be guardians of what other people called 'our heritage'. She was disappointed that this character with a face like a cobweb had not even managed the small task of leaving his Rembrandts on the wall where he found them.

Anne continued to play along until the arrival of Vijay Shah. Only an acquaintance, not a friend of Victor's, they had met ten years before when Vijay, as head of the Debating Society, had invited Victor down to Eton to defend the 'relevance' of philosophy. Since then Vijay had cultivated the connection with a barrage of arty postcards and they had occasionally met at parties in London. Like Victor, Vijay had been an Eton scholar, but unlike Victor he was also very rich.

Anne felt guilty at first that she reacted so badly to Vijay's appearance. His oyster-coloured complexion and the thick jowls that looked like a permanent attack of mumps were the unhappy setting for a large hooked nose with tufts of intractable hair about the nostrils. His glasses were thick and square but, without them, the raw dents on the bridge of his nose and the weak eyes peering out from the darker grey of their sockets looked worse. His hair was blow-dried until it rose and stiffened like a black meringue on top of his skull. His clothes did nothing to compensate for these natural disadvantages. If Vijay's favourite flared green trousers were a mistake, it was a trivial one compared to his range of lightweight jackets in chaotic tartan patterns, with flapless pockets sewn onto the outside. Still, any clothes were preferable to the sight of him in a bathing suit. Anne remembered with horror his narrow shoulders and their white pustules struggling to break through a thick pelt of wiry black hair.

Had Vijay's character been more attractive his appearance might have elicited pity or even indifference, but spending just a few days with him convinced Anne that each hideous feature had been moulded by internal malevolence. His wide, grinning mouth was at once crude and cruel. When he tried to smile, his purplish lips could only curl and twist like a rotting leaf thrown onto a fire. Obsequious and giggly with older and more powerful people, he turned savage at the smell of weakness, and would attack only easy prey. His voice seemed to be designed exclusively for simpering and yet when they had argued on the night before he left, it had achieved the shrill astringency of a betrayed schoolmaster. Like many flatterers, he was not aware that he irritated the people he flattered. When he had met the Wooden Duke he had poured himself out in a rich gurgling rush of compliments, like an overturned bottle of syrup. She overheard George complaining afterwards to David, 'Perfectly ghastly man your friend Victor brought over. Kept telling me about the plaster-work at Richfield. Thought he must want a job as a guide.' George grunted disdainfully and David grunted disdainfully back.

A little Indian guy being sneered at by monsters of English privilege would normally have unleashed the full weight of Anne's loyalty to underdogs, but this time it was wiped out by Vijay's enormous desire to be a monster of English privilege himself. 'I can't bear going to Calcutta,' he giggled, 'the people, my dear, and the noise.' He paused to let everyone appreciate this nonchalant remark made by an English soldier at the Somme.

The memory of Vijay's ingratiating purr died away as Anne tried to push open her bedroom door, which always stuck on a bulge in the quaintly uneven floor. This was another relic of Elaine, who had refused to change what she called 'the authentic feel of the house'. Now the hexagonal tiles were worn to a paler terracotta where the door scraped them each time it was opened. Afraid of spilling her coffee she let the door stay stuck and edged sideways into the room. Her breasts brushed the cupboard as she passed.

Anne put her coffee mug down on the round marble-topped table with black metal legs which Elaine had carried back in triumph from some junk store in Apt and cunningly used as a bedside table. It was far too high and Anne often pulled the wrong book from the pile of unseen titles above her. Suetonius' *Twelve Caesars*, which David had lent her way back at the beginning of August, kept turning up like a reproach. She had glanced at one or two chapters, but the fact that David had recommended the book made her reluctant to become intimate with it. She knew she really ought to read a bit more of it before dinner so as to have something intelligent to say when she gave it back to him tonight. All she remembered was that Caligula had planned to torture his wife to find out why he was so devoted to her. What was David's excuse, she wondered.

Anne lit a cigarette. Lying on a pile of pillows and smaller cushions, slurping her coffee and playing with her cigarette smoke, she felt briefly that her thoughts were growing more subtle and expansive. The only thing that compromised her pleasure was the sound of running water in Victor's bathroom.

First, he would shave and wipe the remnants of the shaving cream on a clean towel. Then he would plaster his hair as flat as he could, walk to the foot of the stairs and shout, 'Darling.' After a brief pause he would shout it again in his let's-not-play-foolish-games voice. If she still did not appear he would call out, 'Breakfast.'

Anne had teased him about it just the other day, and said, 'Oh, darling, you shouldn't have.'

'Have what?'

'Made breakfast.'

'I haven't.'

'Oh, I thought when you shouted, "Breakfast," you meant it was ready.'

'No, I meant that I was ready for breakfast.'

Anne had not been far wrong, Victor was indeed in his bathroom downstairs brushing his hair vigorously. But, as always, a few seconds after he stopped the wave of hair which had tormented him since childhood sprang up again.

His pair of ivory hairbrushes had no handles. They were quite inconvenient, but very traditional, like the wooden bowl of shaving soap, which never thickened as satisfactorily as foam from a can. Victor was fifty-seven, but looked younger. Only a drooping in his flesh, a loss of tension around the jaw and the mouth and the tremendous depth of the horizontal lines in his forehead, revealed his age. His teeth were neat and strong and yellow. Though he longed for something more aerodynamic his nose was bulbous and friendly. Women always praised his eyes because their pale grey looked luminous against his slightly pitted olive-brown skin. All in all, strangers were surprised when a rapid and rather fruity lisp emerged from a face which could well have belonged to an overdressed prizefighter.

In pink pyjamas from New & Lingwood, a silk dressing gown, and a pair of red slippers, Victor felt almost sleek. He had walked out of the bathroom, through his simple whitewashed bedroom with its green mosquito netting held in place over the windows by drawing pins, and out into the kitchen, where he hovered, not yet daring to call Anne.

While Victor hesitated in the kitchen, Eleanor arrived. The Buick was too long to twist its way up Victor's narrow drive and she'd had to park it on the edge of a small pine wood at the bottom of the hill. This land did not belong to Victor but his neighbours, the Fauberts, well known in Lacoste for their eccentric way of life. They still used a mule to plough their fields, they had no electricity, and in their large dilapidated farmhouse they lived in just one room. The rest of the house was crowded with barrels of wine, jars of olive oil, sacks of animal feed, and piles of almonds and lavender. The Fauberts had not altered anything since old Madame Faubert died, and she had never changed anything since she arrived as a young bride, half a century before, bearing a glass bowl and a clock.

Eleanor was intrigued by these people. She imagined their austere and fruitful life like a stained-glass window in a medieval church – labourers in the vineyard with grape-filled baskets on their backs. She had seen one of the Fauberts in the Crédit Agricole and he had the sullen air of a man who looks forward to strangling poultry. Nevertheless, she treasured the idea that the Fauberts were connected to the earth in some wholesome way that the rest of us had forgotten. She had certainly forgotten about being wholesomely connected with the earth herself. Perhaps you had to be a Red Indian, or something.

She tried to walk more slowly up the hill. God, her mind was racing, racing in neutral, she was pouring with sweat and getting flashes of dread through the exhilaration. Balance was so elusive: either it was like this, too fast, or there was the heavy thing like wading through a swamp to get to the end of a sentence. When there were cicadas earlier in the summer it was good.

Their singing was like blood rushing in her ears. It was one of those outside inside things.

Just before the top of the hill she stopped, breathed deeply, and tried to muster her scattered sense of calm, like a bride checking her veil in the last mirror before the aisle. The feeling of solemnity deserted her almost immediately and a few yards further on her legs began to shake. The muscles in her cheeks twitched back like stage curtains, and her heart tried to somersault its way out of her chest. She must remember not to take so many of those yellow pills at once. What on earth had happened to the tranquillizers? They seemed to have been drowned by the floodtide of Dexedrine. Oh, my God, there was Victor in the kitchen, dressed like an advertisement as usual. She gave him a breezy and confident wave through the window.

Victor had finally summoned the courage to call Anne, when he heard the sound of feet on the gravel outside and saw Eleanor waving at him eagerly. Jumping up and down, crossing and uncrossing her arms above her head, her lank blonde hair bobbing from side to side, she looked like a wounded marine trying to attract a helicopter.

She formed the word 'Hello' silently and with great exaggeration as if she were speaking to a deaf foreigner.

'It's open,' Victor called.

One really has to admire her stamina, he thought, moving towards the front door.

Anne, primed to hear the cry of 'Breakfast', was surprised to hear 'It's open' instead. She got out of bed and ran downstairs to greet Eleanor.

'How are you? I'm not even dressed yet.'

'I'm wide awake,' said Eleanor.

'Hello, darling, why don't you make a pot of tea,' said Victor. 'Would you like some, Eleanor?'

'No, thanks.'

After making the tea, Anne went up to dress, pleased that Eleanor had arrived early. Nevertheless, having seen her frenzied air and the sweat-streaked face powder, Anne did not look forward to being driven by her, and she tried to think of some way to do the driving herself.

In the kitchen, with a cigarette dangling from her mouth, Eleanor rummaged about in her handbag for a lighter. She still had her dark glasses on and it was hard to make out the objects in the murky chaos of her bag. Five or six caramel-coloured plastic tubs of pills swirled around with spare packets of Player's cigarettes, a blue leather telephone book, pencils, lipstick, a gold powder compact, a small silver hip-flask full of Fernet-Branca, and a dry-cleaning ticket from Jeeves in Pont Street. Her anxious hands dredged up every object in her bag, except the red plastic lighter she knew was in there somewhere. 'God. I must be going mad,' she muttered.

'I thought I'd take Anne to Signes for lunch,' she said brightly.

'Signes? That's rather out of your way, isn't it?'

'Not the way we're going.' Eleanor had not meant to sound facetious.

'Quite,' Victor smiled tolerantly. 'The way you're going it couldn't be closer, but isn't it rather a long route?'

'Yes, only Nicholas's plane doesn't get in until three and the cork forests are so pretty.' It was unbelievable, there was the dry-cleaning ticket again. There must be more than one. 'And there's that monastery to see, but I don't suppose there'll be time. Patrick always wants to go to the Wild West funfair when we drive that way to the airport. We could stop there too.' Rummage, rummage, rummage, pills, pills, pills. 'I must take him one day. Ah, there's my lighter. How's the book going, Victor?'

'Oh, you know,' said Victor archly, 'identity is a big subject.'

'Does Freud come into it?'

Victor had had this conversation before and if anything made him want to write his book it was the desire
not to have it again. 'I'm not dealing with the subject
from a psychoanalytical point of view.'

'Oh,' said Eleanor, who had lit her cigarette and was
prepared to be fascinated for a while, 'I would have
thought it was – what's the word? – well, terribly
psychological. I mean, if anything's in the mind, it's who
you are.'

'I may quote you on that,' said Victor. 'But remind
me, Eleanor, is the woman Nicholas is bringing this
time his fourth or fifth wife?'

It was no use. She felt stupid again. She always felt
stupid with David and his friends, even when she knew
it was they who were being stupid. 'She's not his wife,'
she said. 'He's left Georgina who was number three,
but he hasn't married this one yet. She's called Bridget.
I think we met in London, but she didn't make a very
strong impression on me.' Anne came downstairs wearing a white cotton dress almost indistinguishable from
the white cotton nightgown she had taken off. Victor
reflected with satisfaction that she still looked young
enough to get away with such a girlish dress. White
dresses deepened the deceptive serenity which her wide
face and high cheekbones and calm black eyes already

gave to her appearance. She stepped lightly into the room. By contrast, Eleanor made Victor think of Lady Wishfort's remark, 'Why I am arrantly flayed; I look like an old peeled wall.'

'OK,' said Anne, 'I guess we can leave whenever you like.

'Will you be all right for lunch?' she asked Victor.

'You know what philosophers are like, we don't notice that kind of thing. And I can always go down to the Cauquière for a rack of lamb with *sauce Béarnaise*.'

'*Béarnaise*? With lamb?' said Anne.

'Of course. The dish which left the poor Duc de Guermantes so famished that he had no time to chat with the dying Swann's dubious daughter before hurrying off to dinner.'

Anne smiled at Eleanor and asked, 'Do you get Proust for breakfast round at your house?'

'No, but we get him for dinner fairly often,' Eleanor replied.

After the two women had said goodbye, Victor turned towards the refrigerator. He had the whole day free to get on with his work and suddenly felt tremendously hungry.

4

'God, I feel awful,' groaned Nicholas, switching on his bedside table lamp.

'Poor squirrel,' said Bridget sleepily.

'What are we doing today? I can't remember.'

'Going to the South of France.'

'Oh yes. What a nightmare. What time's the plane?'

'Twelve something. It arrives at three something. I think there's an hour difference, or something.'

'For Christ sake, stop saying "something".'

'Sorry.'

'God knows why we stayed so late last night. That woman on my right was utterly appalling. I suppose somebody told her long ago that she had a pretty chin, and so she decided to get another one, and another, and another. You know, she used to be married to George Watford.'

'To who?' asked Bridget.

'The one you saw in Peter's photograph album last weekend with a face like a crème brûlée after the first blow of the spoon, all covered in little cracks.'

'Not everyone can have a lover who's rich *and* beautiful,' said Bridget, sliding through the sheets towards him.

'Oaw, give over, luv, give over,' said Nicholas in what he imagined to be a Geordie accent. He rolled out of bed and, moaning, 'Death and destruction,' crawled histrionically across the crimson carpet towards the open door of the bathroom.

Bridget looked critically at Nicholas's body as he clambered to his feet. He had got a lot fatter in the past year. Maybe older men were not the answer. Twenty-three years was a big difference and at twenty, Bridget had not yet caught the marriage fever that tormented the older Watson-Scott sisters as they galloped towards the thirtieth year of their scatterbrained lives. All Nicholas's friends were such wrinklies and some of them were a real yawn. You couldn't exactly drop acid with Nicholas. Well, you could; in fact, she had, but it wasn't the same as with Barry. Nicholas didn't have the right music, the right clothes, the right attitude.

She felt quite bad about Barry, but a girl had to keep her options open.

The thing about Nicholas was that he really was rich and beautiful *and* he was a baronet, which was nice and sort of Jane Austeny. Still, it wouldn't be long before people started saying, 'You can tell he used to be good-looking,' and someone else would intervene charitably with, 'Oh, no, he still is.' In the end she would probably marry him and she would be the fourth Lady Pratt. Then she could divorce him and get half a million pounds, or whatever, and keep Barry as her sex slave and still call herself Lady Pratt in shops. God, sometimes she was so cynical it was frightening.

She knew that Nicholas thought it was the sex that kept them together. It was certainly what had got them together at the party where they first met. Nicholas had been quite drunk and asked her if she was a 'natural blonde'. Yawn, yawn, *what* a tacky question. Still, Barry was in Glastonbury and she'd been feeling a bit restless and so she gave him this heavy look and said, 'Why don't you find out for yourself?' as she slipped out of the room. He thought he *had* found out, but what he didn't know was that she dyed *all* her hair. If you do something cosmetic, you might as well do it thoroughly, that was her motto.

In the bathroom, Nicholas stuck out his tongue and admired its thickly coated surface, still tinged with blackish purple from last night's coffee and red wine. It was all very well to make jokes about Sarah Watford's double chins, but the truth was that unless he held his head up like a Guardsman on parade he had one himself. He couldn't face shaving, but he dabbed on a little of Bridget's make-up. One didn't want to look like the old queen in *Death in Venice*, with rouge trickling down cholera-fevered cheeks, but without a little light powder he had what people called 'a distinctly unhealthy pallor'. Bridget's make-up was rather basic, like her sometimes truly appalling clothes. Whatever one said about Fiona (and one had said some thoroughly unpleasant things in one's time) she did have the most amazing creams and masks sent over from Paris. He sometimes wondered if Bridget might not be (one had to slip into the softening nuances of the French tongue) *insortable*. Last weekend at Peter's she had spent the whole of Sunday lunch giggling like a fourteen-year-old.

And then there was her background. He did not know when the house of Watson and the house of Scott had seen fit to unite their fortunes, but he could tell at a glance that the Watson-Scotts were Old Vicarage material who would kill to have their daughter's engagement in *Country Life*. The father was fond of the races and when Nicholas had taken him and his keen-on-roses wife to *Le Nozze di Figaro* at Covent Garden, Roddy Watson-Scott had said, 'They're under starter's orders,' as the conductor mounted the podium. If the Watson-Scotts were just a little too obscure, at least everyone was agreed that Bridget was flavour of the month and he was a lucky dog to have her.

If he married again he would not choose a girl like Bridget. Apart from anything else, she was completely ignorant. She had 'done' *Emma* for A-level, but since then, as far as he could make out, she only read illus-trated magazines called *Oz* or *The Furry Freak Brothers* supplied to her by a seamy character called Barry. She spent hours poring over pictures of spiralling eyeballs and exploding intestines and policemen with the faces of Doberman pinschers. His own intestines were in a state of bitter confusion and he wanted to clear Bridget out of the bedroom before *they* exploded.

'Darling!' he shouted, or rather tried to shout. The sound came out as a croak. He cleared his throat and spat in the basin.

'You couldn't be an angel and get my glass of orange juice from the dining room, could you? And a cup of tea?'

'Oh, all right.'

Bridget had been lying on her stomach, playing with herself lazily. She rolled out of bed with an exaggerated sigh. God, Nicholas was boring. What was the point of having servants? He treated them better than he treated her. She slouched off to the dining room.

Nicholas sat down heavily on the teak lavatory seat. The thrill of educating Bridget socially and sexually had begun to pall when he had stopped thinking about how wonderfully good he was at it and noticed how little she was willing to learn. After this trip to France he would have to go to Asprey's to get her a going-away present. And yet he did not feel ready for that girl from the Old Masters department of Christie's – a simple string of pearls about her woolly blue neck – who longed to exhaust herself helping a chap to keep his estate intact; a general's daughter used to an atmosphere of discipline. A girl, his thoughts expanded gloomily, who would enjoy the damp little hills of Shropshire's Welsh border, something he had yet to achieve himself despite owning so very many of them and having 'farmer' next to his still unsuccessful candidature for Pratt's club. The Wits never tired of saying, 'But, Nicholas, I thought you owned the place.' He'd made too many enemies to get himself elected.

Nicholas's bowels exploded. He sat there sweating miserably like one of the paranoid wrecks in Bridget's favourite cartoon strips. He could imagine Fattie Poole squealing, 'The man's an absolute cunt, and if they let him in here, I shall have to spend the rest of my life at the Turf.' It had been a mistake to get David Melrose to propose him, but David had been one of his father's best friends, and ten years ago he'd not been as misanthropic or unpopular as he was now, nor had he spent so much time in Lacoste.

The route from Clabon Mews to Heathrow was too familiar to register on Nicholas's senses. He had moved into the soporific phase of his hangover, and felt slightly nauseous. Very tired, he slouched in the corner of the taxi. Bridget was less jaded about foreign travel. Nicholas had taken her to Greece in July and Tuscany in August, and she still liked the idea of how glamorous her life had become.

She disliked Nicholas's English Abroad outfits, particularly the panama hat he had on today and wore tilted over his face to show that he was not in the mood to talk. Nor did she like his off-white wild-silk jacket and the yellow corduroy trousers. She was embarrassed by the shirt with very narrow dark red stripes and a stiff white rounded collar, and by his highly polished shoes. He was a complete freak about shoes. He had fifty pairs, all made for him, and *literally* identical, except for silly details which he treated as world-shatteringly important.

On the other hand, she knew that her own clothes were devastatingly sexy. What could be more sexy than a purple miniskirt and black suede cowboy jacket with tassels hanging all along the arms and across the back? Under the jacket you could see her nipples through the black T-shirt. Her black and purple cowboy boots took half an hour to get off, but they were well worth it, because everybody noticed them.

Since half the time she didn't get the point of one's stories at all, Nicholas wondered whether to tell Bridget about the figs. In any case, he was not sure he wanted her to get the point of the fig story. It had happened about ten years ago, just after David persuaded Eleanor to buy the house in Lacoste. They hadn't married because of Eleanor's mother trying to stop them, and David's father threatening to disinherit him.

Nicholas tipped the brim of his hat. 'Have I ever told you what happened the first time I went to Lacoste?' To make sure the story did not fall flat, he added, 'The place we're going today.'

'No,' said Bridget dully. More stories about people she didn't know, most of them taking place before she was born. Yawn, yawn.

'Well, Eleanor – whom you met at Annabel's, you probably don't remember.'

'The drunk one.'

'Yes!' Nicholas was delighted by these signs of recognition. 'At any rate, Eleanor – who wasn't drunk in those days, just very shy and nervous – had recently bought the house in Lacoste, and she complained to David about the terrible waste of figs that fell from the tree and rotted on the terrace. She mentioned them again the next day when the three of us were sitting outside. I saw a cold look come over David's face. He stuck his lower lip out – always a bad sign, half brutal and half pouting – and said, "Come with me." It felt like following the headmaster to his study. He marched us towards the fig tree with great long strides, Eleanor and I stumbling along behind. When we got there we saw figs scattered all over the stone paving. Some of them were old and squashed, others had broken open, with wasps dancing around the wound or gnawing at the sticky red and white flesh. It was a huge tree and there were a *lot* of figs on the ground. And, then David did this amazing thing. *He told Eleanor to get on all fours and eat all the figs off the terrace.*'

'What, in front of you?' said Bridget, round-eyed.

'Quite. Eleanor *did* look rather confused and I suppose the word is betrayed. She didn't protest, though, just got on with this rather unappetizing task. David wouldn't let her leave a single one. She did once look up pleadingly and say, "I've had enough now, David," but he put his foot on her back and said, "Eat them up. We don't want them going to waste, do we?"'

'Kink-ky,' said Bridget.

Nicholas was rather pleased with the effect his story was having on Bridget. A hit, a palpable hit, he thought to himself.

'What did you do?' asked Bridget.

'I watched,' said Nicholas. 'You don't cross David when he's in that sort of mood. After a while Eleanor looked a little sick and so then I did suggest we collect the rest of the figs in a basket. "You mustn't interfere," said David. "Eleanor can't bear to see the figs wasted when there are starving people in the world. Can you, darling? And so she's going to eat them all up on her own." He grinned at me, and added, "Anyway, she's far too picky about her food, don't you think?"'

'Wow!' said Bridget. 'And you still go and stay with these people?'

The taxi drew up outside the terminal and Nicholas was able to avoid the question. A porter in a brown uniform spotted him immediately and hurried to collect the bags. Nicholas stood transfixed for a moment, like a man under a warm shower, between the grateful cabbie and the assiduous porter, both calling him 'Guv' simultaneously. He always gave larger tips to people who called him 'Guv'. He knew it, and they knew it, it was what was called a 'civilized arrangement'.

Bridget's concentration span was enormously improved by the story about the figs. Even when they had boarded the plane and found their seats, she could still remember what it was she'd wanted him to explain.

'Why do you like this guy anyway? I mean, does he sort of make a habit of ritual humiliation or something?'

'Well, I'm told, although I didn't witness this myself, that he used to make Eleanor take lessons from a prostitute.'

'You're kidding,' said Bridget admiringly. She swivelled round in her seat. 'Kink-ky.'

An air hostess brought two glasses of champagne, apologizing for the slight delay. She had blue eyes and

freckles and smiled ingratiatingly at Nicholas. He preferred these vaguely pretty girls on Air France to the
absurd ginger-haired stewards and frumpish nannies
on English aeroplanes. He felt another wave of tired-
ness from the processed air, the slight pressure on his
ears and eyelids, the deserts of biscuit-coloured plastic
around him and the dry acid taste of the champagne.

The excitement radiating from Bridget revived him a
little, and yet he had still not explained what attracted
him to David. Nor was it a question he particularly
wanted to look into. David was simply part of the
world that counted for Nicholas. One might not like
him, but he was impressive. By marrying Eleanor he
had obliterated the poverty which constituted his great
social weakness. Until recently the Melroses had given
some of the best parties in London.

Nicholas lifted his chin from the cushion of his neck.
He wanted to feed Bridget's ingenuous appetite for the
atmosphere of perversion. Her reaction to the story
about the figs had opened up possibilities he would not
know how to exploit, but even the possibilities were
stimulating.

'You see,' he said to Bridget, 'David was a younger
friend of my father's, and I'm a younger friend of his.
He used to come down to see me at school and take

me to Sunday lunch at the Compleat Angler.' Nicholas could feel Bridget's interest slipping away in the face of this sentimental portrait. 'But what I think fascinated me was the air of doom he carried around with him. As a boy he played the piano brilliantly and then he developed rheumatism and couldn't play,' said Nicholas. 'He won a scholarship to Balliol but left after a month. His father made him join the army and he left that too. He qualified as a doctor but didn't bother to practise. As you can see, he suffers from an almost heroic restlessness.'

'Sounds like a real drag,' said Bridget.

The plane edged slowly towards the runway, while the cabin crew mimed the inflation of life jackets.

'Even their son is the product of rape.' Nicholas watched for her reaction. 'Although you mustn't tell anyone that. I only know because Eleanor told me one evening, when she was very drunk and weepy. She'd been refusing to go to bed with David for ages because she couldn't bear to be touched by him, and then one evening he rugby tackled her on the stairs and wedged her head between the banisters. In law, of course, there is no such thing as marital rape, but David is a law to himself.'

The engines started to roar. 'You'll find in the course

of your life,' boomed Nicholas, and then, realizing that he sounded pompous, he put on his funny pompous voice, 'as I have found in the course of mine, that such people, though perhaps destructive and cruel towards those who are closest to them, often possess a vitality that makes other people seem dull by comparison.'

'Oh, God, gimme a break,' said Bridget. The plane gathered speed and shuddered into the pasty English sky.

5

As Eleanor's Buick drifted along the slow back roads to Signes the sky was almost clear except for a straggling cloud dissolving in front of the sun. Through the tinted border of the windscreen, Anne saw the cloud's edges curling and melting in the heat. The car had already been caught behind an orange tractor, its trailer loaded with dusty purple grapes; the driver had waved them on magnanimously. Inside the car, the air conditioning gently refrigerated the atmosphere. Anne had tried to prise the keys from her, but Eleanor said that nobody else ever drove her car. Now the soft suspension and streams of cold air made the dangers of her driving seem more remote.

It was still only eleven o'clock and Anne was not looking forward to the long day ahead. There had been an awkward, stale silence since she'd made the mistake of asking how Patrick was. Anne felt a maternal instinct towards him, which was more than she could say for his mother. Eleanor had snapped at her, 'Why do people think they are likely to please me by asking how Patrick is, or how David is? I don't know how they are, only they know.'

Anne was stunned. A long time went by before Anne tried again. 'What did you think of Vijay?'

'Not much.'

'Me neither. Luckily he had to leave earlier than expected.' Anne still did not know how much to reveal about the row with Vijay. 'He was going to stay with that old man they all worship, Jonathan somebody, who writes those awful books with the crazy titles, like *Anemones and Enemies* or *Antics and Antiques*. You know the one I mean?'

'Oh, him, Jesus, he's awful. He used to come to my mother's house in Rome. He would always say things like, "The streets are pullulating with beggars," which made me really angry when I was sixteen. But is that Vijay man rich? He kept talking as if he must be, but he didn't look as if he ever spent any money – not on his clothes anyhow?'

'Oh, yeah,' said Anne, 'he is *so* rich: he is factory-rich, bank-rich. He keeps polo ponies in Calcutta, but he doesn't like polo and never goes to Calcutta. Now that's what I call rich.'

Eleanor was silent for a while. It was a subject in which she felt quietly competitive. She did not want to agree too readily that neglecting polo ponies in Calcutta was what she called rich.

'But stingy as hell,' said Anne to cover the silence. 'That was one of the reasons we had a row.' She was longing to tell the truth now, but she was still unsure. 'Every evening he rang home, which is Switzerland, to chat in Gujarati to his aged mother, and if there was no answer, he'd show up in the kitchen with a black shawl around his frail shoulders, looking like an old woman himself. Finally I had to ask him for some money for the phone calls.'

'And did he pay you?'

'Only after I lost my temper.'

'Didn't Victor help?' asked Eleanor.

'Victor shies away from crass things like money.'

The road had cut into cork forests, and trees with old or fresh wounds where belts of bark had been stripped from their trunks grew thickly on both sides.

'Has Victor been doing much writing this summer?' asked Eleanor.

'Hardly any. And it's not as if he does anything else

when he's at home,' Anne replied. 'You know, he's been coming down here for what? Eight years? And he's never even been over to say hello to those farmers next door.'

'The Fauberts?'

'Right. Not once. They live three hundred yards away in that old farmhouse, with the two cypresses out front. Victor's garden practically belongs to them, but they've never exchanged a word. "We haven't been introduced," is his excuse,' said Anne.

'He's terribly English for an Austrian, isn't he?' smiled Eleanor. 'Oh look, we're coming up to Signes. I hope I can find that funny restaurant. It's in a square opposite one of those fountains that's turned into a mound of wet moss with ferns growing out of it. And inside there are heads of wild boars with polished yellow tusks all over the walls. Their mouths are painted red, so it looks as if they could still charge out from behind the wall.'

'God, how terrifying,' said Anne, drily.

'When the Germans left here,' Eleanor continued, 'at the end of the war, they shot every man in the village, except for Marcel – the one who owns the restaurant. He was away when it happened.'

Anne was silenced by Eleanor's air of crazed

empathy. Once they'd found the restaurant, she was at once relieved and a little disappointed that the dark watery square was not more redolent of sacrifice and retribution. The walls of the restaurant were made of blonde plastic moulded to look like planks of pine and there were in fact only two boars' heads in the rather empty room, which was harshly lit by bare fluorescent tubes. After the first course of tiny thrushes full of lead shot and trussed up on pieces of greasy toast, Anne could only toy with the dark depressing stew, loaded onto a pile of overcooked noodles. The red wine was cold and raw and came in old green bottles with no label.

'Great place, isn't it?' said Eleanor.

'It's certainly got atmosphere,' said Anne.

'Look, there's Marcel,' said Eleanor desperately.

'*Ah, Madame Melrose, je ne vous ai pas vue,*' he said, pretending to notice Eleanor for the first time. He hurried round the end of the bar with quick small steps, wiping his hands on the stained white apron. Anne noticed his drooping moustache and the extraordinary bags under his eyes.

Immediately, he offered Eleanor and Anne some cognac. Anne refused despite his claim that it would do her good, but Eleanor accepted, and then returned the offer. They drank another and chatted about the grape harvest while Anne, who could only understand a little of his *midi* accent, regretted even more that she was not allowed to drive.

By the time they got back to the car, the cognac and tranquillizers had come into their own and Eleanor felt her blood tumbling like ball bearings through the veins under her numbed skin. Her head was as heavy as a sack of coins and she closed her eyes slowly, slowly, completely in control.

'Hey,' said Anne, 'wake up.'

'I am awake,' said Eleanor grumpily and then more serenely, 'I'm awake.' Her eyes remained closed.

'Please let me drive.' Anne was ready to argue the point.

'Sure,' said Eleanor. She opened her eyes, which suddenly seemed intensely blue against the pinkish tinge of frayed blood vessels. 'I trust you.'

Eleanor slept for about half an hour while Anne drove up and down the twisting roads from Signes to Marseilles.

When Eleanor woke up, she was lucid again and said, 'Goodness that stew was awfully rich, I did feel a little weighed down after lunch.' The high from the Dexedrine was back; like the theme from *The Valkyrie*, it could not be kept down for long, even if it took a more muted and disguised form than before.

'What's Le Wild Ouest?' said Anne. 'I keep passing pictures of cowboys with arrows through their hats.'

'Oh, we must go, we must go,' said Eleanor in a childish voice. 'It's a funfair but the whole thing is made to look like Dodge City. I've never actually been in, but I'd really like to—'

'Have we got time?' asked Anne sceptically.

'Oh, yes, it's only one-thirty, look, and the airport is only forty-five minutes away. Oh, let's. Just for half an hour. Pl-ea-se?'

Another billboard announced Le Wild Ouest at four hundred metres. Soaring above the tops of the dark pine trees were miniature imitation stagecoaches in brightly coloured plastic hanging from a stationary Ferris wheel.

'This can't be for real,' said Anne. 'Isn't it fantastic? We have to go in.'

They walked through the giant saloon doors of Le Wild Ouest. On either side, the flags of many nations drooped on a circle of white poles.

'Gosh, it's exciting,' said Eleanor. It was hard for her to decide which of the wonderful rides to take first. In the end she chose to go on the stagecoach Ferris wheel. 'I want a yellow one,' she said.

The wheel edged forward as each stagecoach was filled. Eventually, theirs rose above the level of the highest pines.

'Look! There's our car,' squealed Eleanor.

'Does Patrick like this place?' asked Anne.

'He's never been,' said Eleanor.

'You'd better take him soon, or he'll be too old. People grow out of this sort of thing, you know.' Anne smiled.

Eleanor looked massively gloomy for a moment. The wheel started to turn, generating a little breeze. On the upward curve, Eleanor felt her stomach tighten. Instead of giving her a better view of the funfair and the surrounding woods, the motion of the wheel made her feel sick and she stared grimly at the white tips of her knuckles, longing for the ride to be over.

Anne saw that Eleanor's mood had snapped and that she was again in the company of an older, richer, drunker woman.

They got off the ride, and walked through a street of shooting arcades. 'Let's get out of this fucking place,' said Eleanor. 'It's time to collect Nicholas anyhow.'

'So tell me about Nicholas,' said Anne, trying to keep up.

'Oh, you'll find out soon enough.'

6

'So this Eleanor woman is a real victim, right?' said Bridget. She had fallen asleep after smoking a joint in the loo and she wanted to compensate with a burst of belated curiosity.

'Is every woman who chooses to live with a difficult man a victim?'

Nicholas undid his seatbelt as soon as the plane landed. They were in the second row and could easily get off ahead of the other passengers if, just for once, Bridget did not unsheathe her compact from its blue velvet pouch and admire herself in its powdery little mirror.

'Shall we go,' sighed Nicholas.

'The seatbelt sign is still on.'

'Signs are for sheep.'

'Bahaha-a-a,' bleated Bridget at the mirror, 'I'm a sheep.'

This woman is intolerable, thought Nicholas.

'Well, I'm a shepherd,' he said out loud, 'and don't make me put on my wolf's clothing.'

'Oh, my,' said Bridget, cowering in the corner of her seat, 'what big teeth you have.'

'All the better to bite your head off.'

'I don't think you're my granny at all,' she said with real disappointment.

The plane stopped its creeping progress and there was a general clicking of opening buckles and discarded seatbelts.

'Come on,' said Nicholas, now all businesslike. He very much disliked joining the struggling tourists as they jostled each other down the aisle.

They arrived at the open door of the plane, pale and overdressed, and started to clank their way down a flight of metal steps, caught between the air crew who pretended to be sorry at their departure and the ground crew who pretended to be pleased by their arrival. As she went down the steps, Bridget felt slightly nauseous from the heat and the smell of spent fuel.

Nicholas looked across the tarmac at the long queue of Arabs slowly climbing on board an Air France plane.

He thought of the Algerian crisis in '62 and the threat of betrayed colonists parachuting into Paris. The thought petered out as he imagined how far back he would have to begin in order to explain it to Bridget. She probably thought that Algeria was an Italian dress designer. He felt a familiar longing for a well-informed woman in her early thirties who had read history at Oxford; the fact that he had divorced two of them already made little difference to his immediate enthusiasm. Their flesh might hang more loosely on the bone, but the memory of intelligent conversation tormented him like the smell of succulent cooking wafting into a forgotten prison cell. Why was the centre of his desire always in a place he had just deserted? He knew that the memory of Bridget's flesh would betray him with the same easy poignancy if he were now climbing on to the bus with a woman whose conversation he could bear. Theoretically, of course, there were women – he had even had affairs with them – who combined the qualities which he threw into unnecessary competition, but he knew that something inside him would always scatter his appreciation and divide his loyalties.

The doors folded shut and the bus jerked into motion. Bridget sat opposite Nicholas. Under her absurd skirt, her legs were slim and bare and golden. He detached them pornographically from the rest of her body, and found he was still excited by the idea of their availability. He crossed his legs and loosened his entangled boxer shorts through the stiff ridges of his corduroy trousers.

It was only when he considered to whom these golden legs belonged that his fleeting erection seemed a small and inconvenient reward for a state of almost permanent irritation. In fact, scanning the figure above the waist, along the fringed sleeve of her black suede jacket, and up towards the bored and stubborn expression on her face, he felt a spasm of revulsion and estrangement. Why was he taking this ludicrous creature to stay with David Melrose who was, after all, a man of some discernment, not to say a merciless snob?

The terminal building smelled of disinfectant. A woman in blue overalls drifted across the glaring floor, the circular pads of her polishing machine humming as she swung it gently back and forth across the black and brown translucent pebbles trapped in cheap white marble. Still stoned, Bridget lost herself in the flakes of colour as if they were the flint and quartz stars of a white sky.

'What are you staring at?' snapped Nicholas.

'This floor is something else,' said Bridget.

At passport control she could not find her passport but Nicholas refused to start a scene just when they were about to meet Eleanor.

'Rather eccentrically, in this airport one crosses the main lobby before collecting one's luggage,' said Nicholas. 'That's probably where Eleanor will be waiting for us.'

'Wow!' said Bridget. 'If I was a smuggler,' she paused, hoping Nicholas might challenge her, 'this would be my dream airport. I mean, there's this whole lobby where you could slip someone your hand luggage, full of goodies, and then go and fetch your legal luggage for Customs.'

'That's what I admire about you,' said Nicholas, 'your creative thinking. You might have had a brilliant career in advertising; although I think as far as smuggling goes the Marseilles authorities have more pressing problems to wrestle with than any "goodies" you might import in your handbag. I don't know if you're aware of it but . . .'

Bridget had stopped listening. Nicholas was being a wanker again. He always got like this when he was uptight; in fact he was like this all the time except when he was in bed, or with people he wanted to charm.

Lagging behind, she stuck her tongue out at him. Nyah, nyah, nyah . . . boring, boring, boring.

Bridget covered her ears and looked down at her dragging feet, while Nicholas strode on alone, pouring sarcasm on ideas increasingly remote from Bridget's tame remarks about smuggling.

Looking up again, Bridget saw a familiar figure. It was Barry leaning against the pillar next to the newsstand. Barry could always sense when he was being looked at and, depending on his mood, attributed this to 'paranoia' or 'ESP'.

'Bridge! Incredible!'

'Barry! All you need is love,' said Bridget, reading out loud the words on Barry's T-shirt and laughing.

'This really is incredible,' said Barry, running his fingers through his long black hair. 'You know I was thinking about you this morning.'

Barry thought about Bridget every morning, but it still struck him as further evidence of mind control that he had not only thought about her today but run into her at the airport as well.

'We're going to Arles for the Progressive Jazz Festival,' said Barry. 'Hey, why don't you come along? It's going to be really fantastic. Bux Millerman is playing.'

'Wow,' breathed Bridget.

'Hey, listen,' said Barry, 'take Etienne's number any-way. That's where I'll be staying and maybe we can like meet up.'

'Yeah,' said Bridget, 'great.'

Barry pulled out a giant Rizla rolling paper and scribbled a number on it. 'Don't smoke it,' he said humorously, 'or we'll never get in touch.'

Bridget gave him the Melrose number because she knew he would not use it, and that this whole meeting-up thing was not going to happen. 'How long have you been here?' she asked.

'Ten days roughly and the only piece of advice I can give you is *don't drink the pink*. That wine is full of chemical shit and the hangover is worse than the come-down off a sulphate binge.'

Nicholas's voice burst in on them. 'What the hell do you think you're doing?' He glared at her. 'You're really pushing your luck, swanning off in the middle of an airport without any warning. I've been dragging round these fucking cases looking for you for the last quarter of an hour.'

'You should get a trolley,' said Barry.

Nicholas stared straight ahead of him as if nobody

had spoken. 'Don't ever do this again or I'll snap you like . . . Ah, there's Eleanor!'

'Nicholas, I'm so sorry. We got caught on the Ferris wheel at a funfair and instead of letting us off they sent it round a second time. Can you imagine?'

'So like you, Eleanor, always getting more fun than you bargained for.'

'Well, I'm here now.' Eleanor greeted Nicholas and Bridget with a flat circular wave, like someone polishing a windowpane. 'And this is Anne Moore.'

'Hi,' said Anne.

'How do you do?' said Nicholas, and introduced Bridget.

Eleanor led them towards the car park and Bridget blew a kiss over her shoulder in Barry's direction.

'*Ciao*,' said Barry, jabbing his finger at the confident words on his T-shirt. 'Don't forget.'

'Who was that fascinating-looking man your girl-friend was talking to?' asked Eleanor.

'Oh, just somebody on the plane,' said Nicholas. He was annoyed to find Barry at the airport and for a moment he thought that Bridget might have arranged the meeting. The idea was absurd, but he could not shake it off, and as soon as they were all settled in the car, he hissed at her, 'What were you talking to that chap about?'

'Barry isn't a chap,' said Bridget, 'that's what I like about him, but if you really want to know, he said, "Don't drink the pink, it's full of chemical shit and the hangover is worse than a comedown off a speed binge."'

Nicholas swivelled round and gave her a deadly look.

'He's absolutely right, of course,' said Eleanor. 'Perhaps we should have asked him to dinner.'

7

After hanging Patrick from his ears and watching him escape from the library, David shrugged, sat down at the piano, and started to improvise a fugue. His rheumatic hands protested at every key he touched. A glass of pastis, like a trapped cloud, stood on top of the piano. His body ached all day long and the pain woke him at night every time he shifted position. Nightmares often woke him as well and made him whimper and scream so loudly that his insomnia overflowed into neighbouring bedrooms. His lungs, also, were shot away and when his asthma flared up he wheezed and rattled, his face swollen by the cortisone he used to appease his constricted chest. Gasping, he would pause at the top of the stairs, unable to speak, his eyes roaming over the ground as if he were searching for the air he desperately needed.

At the age of fifteen his musical talent had attracted the interest of the great piano teacher Shapiro, who took on only one pupil at a time. Unfortunately, within a week, David had contracted rheumatic fever and spent the next six months in bed with hands too stiff and clumsy to practise on the piano. The illness wiped out his chances of becoming a serious pianist and, although pregnant with musical ideas, from then on he claimed to be bored by composition and those 'hordes of little tadpoles' one had to use to record music on paper. Instead, he had hordes of admirers who pleaded with him to play after dinner. They always clamoured for the tune they had heard last time, which he could not remember, until they heard the one he played now, which he soon forgot. His compulsion to amuse others and the arrogance with which he displayed his talent combined to disperse the musical ideas he had once guarded so closely and secretly.

Even while he drank in the flattery he knew that underneath this flamboyant frittering away of his talent he had never overcome his reliance on pastiche, his fear of mediocrity, and the rankling suspicion that the first attack of fever was somehow self-induced. This insight was useless to him; to know the causes of his failure did not diminish the failure, but it did make his self-hatred a little more convoluted and a little more lucid than it would have been in a state of plain ignorance.

As the fugue developed, David attacked its main theme with frustrated repetitions, burying the initial melody under a mudslide of rumbling bass notes, and spoiling its progress with violent bursts of dissonance. At the piano he could sometimes abandon the ironic tactics which saturated his speech, and visitors whom he had bullied and teased to the point of exasperation found themselves moved by the piercing sadness of the music in the library. On the other hand, he could turn the piano on them like a machine gun and concentrate a hostility into his music that made them long for the more conventional unkindness of his conversation. Even then, his playing would haunt the people who most wanted to resist his influence.

David stopped playing abruptly and closed the lid over the keyboard. He took a gulp of pastis and started to massage his left palm with his right thumb. This massage made the pain a little worse, but gave him the same psychological pleasure as tearing at scabs, probing abscesses and mouth ulcers with his tongue, and fingering bruises.

When a couple of stabs from his thumb had converted the dull ache in his palm into a sharper sensation, he leaned over and picked up a half-smoked Monte-cristo cigar. One was 'supposed' to remove the paper band from the cigar, and so David left it on. To break even the smallest rules by which others convinced themselves that they were behaving correctly gave him great pleasure. His disdain for vulgarity included the vulgarity of wanting to avoid the appearance of being vulgar. In this more esoteric game, he recognized only a handful of players, Nicholas Pratt and George Watford among them, and he could just as easily despise a man for leaving the band *on* his cigar. He enjoyed watching Victor Eisen, the great thinker, thrashing about in these shallow waters, more firmly hooked each time he tried to cross the line that separated him from the class he yearned to belong to.

David brushed the soft flakes of cigar ash from his blue woollen dressing gown. Every time he smoked he thought of the emphysema that had killed his father, and felt annoyed by the prospect of dying in the same manner.

Under the dressing gown he wore a pair of very faded and much darned pyjamas that had become his on the day his father was buried. The burial had taken place conveniently close to his father's house, in the little churchyard he had spent the last few months of his life staring at through the window of his study. Wearing the oxygen mask which he humorously called his 'gas mask', and unable to negotiate the 'stair drill', he slept in his study, which he renamed the 'departure lounge', on an old Crimean campaign bed left to him by his uncle.

David attended the damp and conventional funeral without enthusiasm; he already knew he had been disinherited. As the coffin was lowered into the ground, he reflected how much of his father's life had been spent in a trench of one sort or another, shooting at birds or men, and how it was really the best place for him.

After the funeral, when the guests had left, David's mother came up to his old bedroom for a moment of private mourning with her son. She said, in her sublime voice, 'I know he would have wanted you to have these,' and placed a pair of carefully folded pyjamas on the bed. When David did not reply, she pressed his hand and closed her faintly blue eyelids for a moment, to show that such things lay too deep for words, but that she knew how much he would prize the little pile of white and yellow flannel from a shop in Bond Street which had gone out of business before the First World War.

It was the same yellow and white flannel that had

now grown too hot. David got up from the piano stool and paced about with his dressing gown open, puffing on his cigar. There was no doubt that he was angry with Patrick for running away. It had spoiled his fun. He granted that he had perhaps miscalculated the amount of discomfort he could safely inflict on Patrick.

David's methods of education rested on the claim that childhood was a romantic myth which he was too clear-sighted to encourage. Children were weak and ignorant miniature adults who should be given every incentive to correct their weakness and their ignorance. Like King Chaka, the great Zulu warrior, who made his troops stamp thorn bushes into the ground in order to harden their feet, a training some of them may well have resented at the time, he was determined to harden the calluses of disappointment and develop the skill of detachment in his son. After all, what else did he have to offer him?

For a moment he was winded by a sense of absurdity and impotence; he felt like a farmer watching a flock of crows settle complacently on his favourite scarecrow.

But he pushed on bravely with his original line of thought. No, it was no use expecting gratitude from Patrick, although one day he might realize, like one of

Chaka's men running over flinty ground on indifferent feet, how much he owed to his father's uncompromising principles.

When Patrick was born David had been worried that he might become a refuge or an inspiration to Eleanor, and he had jealously set about ensuring that this did not happen. Eleanor eventually resigned herself to a vague and luminous faith in Patrick's 'wisdom', a quality she attributed to him some time before he had learned to control his bowels. She thrust him downstream in this paper boat and collapsed back, exhausted by terror and guilt. Even more important to David than the very natural worry that his wife and his son might grow fond of one another was the intoxicating feeling that he had a blank consciousness to work with, and it gave him great pleasure to knead this yielding clay with his artistic thumbs.

As he walked upstairs to get dressed, even David, who spent most of his day angry or at least irritated, and who made a point of not letting things surprise him, was surprised by the burst of rage that swept over him. What had started as indignation at Patrick's escape turned now into a fury he could no longer control. He strode into his bedroom with his underlip pushed out petulantly and his fists clenched, but he felt at the same time a strong desire to escape his own atmosphere, like a crouching man hurrying to get away from the whirling blades of the helicopter in which he has just landed.

The bedroom he entered had a mock-monastic look, large and white, with bare dark-brown tiles miraculously warm in winter when the underfloor heating was turned on. The only painting on the wall was a picture of Christ wearing the crown of thorns, one of which pierced his pale brow. A trickle of still fresh blood ran down his smooth forehead towards his swimming eyes, which looked up diffidently at this extraordinary headgear as if to ask, 'But is it really *me*?' The painting was a Correggio and easily the most valuable object in the house, but David had insisted on hanging it in his bedroom, saying sweetly that he would ask for nothing else.

The brown and gold bedhead, bought by Eleanor's mother, who was by then the Duchesse de Valençay, from a dealer who assured her that Napoleon's head had rested against it on at least one occasion, further compromised the austerity of the room, as did the dark-green silk Fortuny bedspread, covered in phoenixes floating up from the fires beneath them. Curtains of the same fabric hung from a simple wooden pole, at windows which opened onto a balcony with a wrought-iron balustrade.

David opened these windows impatiently and stepped onto the balcony. He looked at the tidy rows of vines, the rectangular fields of lavender, the patches of pine-wood, and beyond to the villages of Bécasse and St-Crau draped over the lower hills. 'Like a couple of ill-fitting skull-caps,' as he liked to say to Jewish friends.

He shifted his gaze upward and scanned the long curved ridge of the mountain which, on a clear day like this, seemed so close and so wild. Searching for something in the landscape that would receive his mood and answer it, he could only think again, as he had so often before, how easy it would be to dominate the whole valley with a single machine gun riveted to the rail which he now gripped with both hands.

He was turning back restlessly towards the bedroom when a movement below the balcony caught the corner of his eye.

Patrick had stayed in his hiding place for as long as he could, but it was cold in there out of the sun and so he scrambled from under the bush and, with theatrical reluctance, started to walk back home through the tall dry grass. To sulk alone was difficult. He felt the need for a wider audience but he wished he didn't. He dared not punish anyone with his absence, because he was not sure that his absence would be noticed.

He walked along slowly, then curved back to the edge of the wall and stopped to stare at the big mountain on the other side of the valley. The massive formations up on the crest and the smaller ones dotted over its sides yielded shapes and faces as he willed them to appear. An eagle's head. A grotesque nose. A party of dwarfs. A bearded old man. A rocket ship, and countless leprous and obese profiles with cavernous eye sockets formed out of the smoky fluidity his concentration gave to the stone. After a while, he no longer recognized what he was thinking and, just as a shop window sometimes prevents the onlooker from seeing the objects behind the glass and folds him instead in a narcissistic embrace, his mind ignored the flow of impressions from the outside world and locked him into a daydream he could not have subsequently described.

The thought of lunch dragged him back into the present with a strong sense of anxiety. What was the time? Was he too late? Would Yvette still be there to talk to him? Would he have to eat alone with his father? He always recovered from his mental truancy with disappointment. He enjoyed the feeling of blankness, but it frightened him afterwards when he came out of it and could not remember what he had been thinking.

Patrick broke into a run. He was convinced that he had missed lunch. It was always at a quarter to two and normally Yvette would come out and call him, but hiding in the bushes he might not have heard.

When he arrived outside the kitchen, Patrick could see Yvette through the open door, washing lettuce in the sink. He had a stitch in his side from running, and now that he could tell that lunch was some way off he felt embarrassed by his desperate haste. Yvette waved to him from the sink, but he did not want to look hurried, so he just waved back and strolled past the door, as if he had business of his own to attend to. He decided to check once more whether he could find the lucky tree frog before doubling back to the kitchen to sit with Yvette.

Around the corner of the house, Patrick climbed up onto the low wall at the outer edge of the terrace and, a fifteen-foot drop to his left, he balanced his way along with arms spread out. He walked the whole length of the wall and then jumped down again. He was at the top of the garden steps with the fig tree in sight, when he heard his father's voice shouting, '*Don't let me ever see you do that again!*'

Patrick was startled. Where was the voice coming from? Was it shouting at him? He spun around and looked behind him. His heart was beating hard. He often overheard his father shouting at other people, especially his mother, and it terrified him and made him want to run away. But this time he had to stand still and listen because he wanted to understand what was wrong and whether he was to blame.

'*Come up here immediately!*'

Now Patrick knew where the voice was coming from. He looked up and saw his father leaning over the balcony.

'What have I done wrong?' he asked, but too quietly to be heard. His father looked so furious that Patrick lost all conviction of his own innocence. With growing alarm he tried to work backward from his father's rage to what his own crime might be.

By the time he had climbed the steep stairs to his father's bedroom, Patrick was ready to apologize for anything, but still felt a lingering desire to know what he was apologizing for. In the doorway he stopped and asked again, audibly this time, 'What have I done wrong?'

'Close the door behind you,' said his father. 'And

come over here.' He sounded disgusted by the obligation the child had thrust upon him.

As Patrick slowly crossed the floor he tried to think of some way to placate his father. Maybe if he said something clever he'd be forgiven, but he felt extraordinarily stupid and could only think over and over: two times two equals four, two times two equals four. He tried to remember something he had noticed that morning, or anything, anything at all that might persuade his father that he had been 'observing everything'. But his mind was eclipsed by the shadow of his father's presence.

He stood by the bed and stared down at the green bedspread with the bonfire birds on it. His father sounded rather weary when he spoke.

'I'm going to have to beat you.'

'*But what have I done wrong?*'

'You know perfectly well what you have done,' his father said in a cold, annihilating voice that Patrick found overwhelmingly persuasive. He was suddenly ashamed of all the things he had done wrong. His whole existence seemed to be contaminated by failure.

Moving quickly, his father grabbed Patrick's shirt collar. He sat down on the bed, hoisted Patrick over his right thigh, and removed the yellow slipper from his left foot. Such rapid manoeuvres would normally have made David wince with pain, but he was able to regain his youthful agility in the service of such a good cause. He pulled down Patrick's trousers and underpants and raised the slipper surprisingly high for a man who had trouble with his right shoulder.

The first blow was astonishingly painful. Patrick tried to take the attitude of stoic misery admired by dentists. He tried to be brave but, during the beating, although he at last realized that his father wanted to hurt him as much as possible, he refused to believe it.

The harder he struggled, the harder he was hit. Longing to move but afraid to move, he was split in half by this incomprehensible violence. Horror closed in on him and crushed his body like the jaws of a dog. After the beating, his father dropped him like a dead thing onto the bed.

And he still could not get away. Pushing his palm against Patrick's right shoulder blade, his father was holding him down. Patrick twisted his head around anxiously, but could only see the blue of his father's dressing gown.

'What are you doing?' he asked, but his father did not answer and Patrick was too scared to repeat the question. His father's hand was pushing down on him and, his face squashed into the folds of the bedspread, he could hardly breathe. He stared fixedly up at the curtain pole and the top of the open windows. He could not understand what form the punishment was now taking, but he knew that his father must be very angry with him to be hurting him so much. He could not stand the helplessness that washed over him. He could not stand the unfairness. He did not know who this man was, it could not be his father who was crushing him like this.

From the curtain pole, if he could get up on the curtain pole, he could have sat looking down on the whole scene, just as his father was looking down on him. For a moment, Patrick felt he was up there watching with detachment the punishment inflicted by a strange man on a small boy. As hard as he could Patrick concentrated on the curtain pole and this time it lasted longer, he was sitting up there, his arms folded, leaning back against the wall.

Then he was back down on the bed again feeling a kind of blankness and bearing the weight of not knowing what was happening. He could hear his father wheezing, and the bedhead bumping against the wall. From behind the curtains with the green birds, he saw a gecko emerge and cling motionlessly to the corner of

the wall beside the open window. Patrick lanced himself towards it. Tightening his fists and concentrating
until his concentration was like a telephone wire
stretched between them, Patrick disappeared into the
lizard's body.

The gecko understood, because at that very instant
it dashed round the corner of the window and out onto
the wall. Below he could see the drop to the terrace
and the leaves of the Virginia creeper, red and green and
yellow, and from up there, close against the wall, he
could hold on with suckered feet and hang upside down
safely from the eaves of the roof. He scurried onto the
old roof tiles which were covered in grey and orange
lichen, and then into the trough between the tiles, all
the way up to the ridge of the roof. He moved fast down
the other slope, and was far away, and nobody would
ever find him again, because they wouldn't know where
to look, and couldn't know that he was coiled up in the
body of a gecko.

'Stay here,' said David, standing up and adjusting his
yellow and white pyjamas.

Patrick could not have done anything else. He
recognized, dully at first and then more vividly, the
humiliation of his position. Face down on the bed, with
his trousers bunched around his knees and a strange,

worrying wetness at the base of his spine. It made him think he was bleeding. That, somehow, his father had stabbed him in the back.

His father went to the bathroom and came back. With a handful of lavatory paper he wiped away the increasingly cold pool of slime that had started to trickle between Patrick's buttocks.

'You can get up now,' he said.

Patrick could not in fact get up. The memory of voluntary action was too remote and complicated. Impatiently, his father pulled up Patrick's trousers and lifted him off the bed. Patrick stood beside the bed while his father clasped his shoulders, ostensibly to straighten his stance, but it made Patrick think that his father was going to pin his shoulders back and force them together until he was turned inside out and his lungs and heart burst out of his chest.

Instead, David leaned over and said, 'Don't ever tell your mother or anyone else what happened today, or you'll be *very* severely punished. Do you understand?'

Patrick nodded.

'Are you hungry?'

Patrick shook his head.

'Well, I'm starving,' said David chattily. 'You really should eat more, you know. Build up your strength.'

'Can I go now?'

'All right, if you don't want any lunch, you can go.' David was irritated again.

Patrick walked down the drive and as he stared at the toes of his scuffed sandals he saw, instead, the top of his head as if from ten or twelve feet in the air, and he felt an uncomfortable curiosity about the boy he was watching. It was not quite personal, like the accident they saw on the road last year and his mother said not to look.

Back down again, Patrick felt utter defeat. There was no flash of purple cloaks. No special soldiers. No gecko. Nothing. He tried to take to the air again, the way seabirds do when a wave breaks over the rock where they were standing. But he had lost the power to move and stayed behind, drowning.

8

During lunch David felt that he had perhaps pushed his disdain for middle-class prudery a little too far. Even at the bar of the Cavalry and Guards Club one couldn't boast about homosexual, paedophiliac incest with any confidence of a favourable reception. Who could he tell that he had raped his five-year-old son? He could not think of a single person who would not prefer to change the subject – and some would behave far worse than that. The experience itself had been short and brutish, but not altogether nasty. He smiled at Yvette, said how ravenous he was, and helped himself to the brochette of lamb and flageolets.

'Monsieur has been playing the piano all morning.'

'And playing with Patrick,' David added piously.

Yvette said they were so exhausting at that age.

'Exhausting!' David agreed.

Yvette left the room and David poured another glass of the Romanée-Conti that he had taken from the cellar for dinner, but had decided to drink on his own. There were always more bottles and it went so well with lamb. 'Nothing but the best, or go without': that was the code he lived by, as long as the 'go without' didn't actually happen. There was no doubt about it, he was a sensualist, and as to this latest episode, he hadn't done anything medically dangerous, just a little rubbing between the buttocks, nothing that would not happen to the boy at school in due course. If he had committed any crime, it was to set about his son's education too assiduously. He was conscious of already being sixty, there was so much to teach him and so little time.

He rang the little bell beside his plate and Yvette came back into the dining room.

'Excellent lamb,' said David.

'Would Monsieur like the tarte Tatin?'

He had no room left, alas, for tarte Tatin. Perhaps she could tempt Patrick to have some for tea. He just wanted coffee. Could she bring it to the drawing room? Of course she could.

David's legs had stiffened and when he rose from his chair he staggered for a couple of steps, drawing in his breath sharply through his teeth. 'God damn,' he said out loud. He had suddenly lost all tolerance for his rheumatic pains and decided to go upstairs to Eleanor's bathroom, a pharmaceutical paradise. He very seldom used painkillers, preferring a steady flow of alcohol and the consciousness of his own heroism.

Opening the cupboard under Eleanor's basin he was struck by the splendour and variety of the tubes and bottles: clear ones and yellow ones and dark ones, orange ones with green caps, in plastic and glass, from half a dozen countries, all urging the consumer not to exceed the stated dose. There were even envelopes marked Seconal and Mandrax, stolen, he imagined, from other people's bathroom cabinets. Rummaging about among the barbiturates and stimulants and anti-depressants and hypnotics, he found surprisingly few painkillers. He had turned up only a bottle of codeine, a few diconol and some distalgesics, when he discovered, at the back of the cupboard, a bottle of sugar-coated opium pellets he had prescribed just two years before, for his mother-in-law, to ease the uncontrollable diarrhoea which accompanied her intestinal cancer. This last act of Hippocratic mercy, long after the end of his brief medical practice, filled him with nostalgia for the healer's art.

On a charmingly quaint label from Harris's in St

James's Street, was written: 'The Opium (B.P. 0.6 grains)' and under that, 'Duchesse de Valençay' and finally, 'To be taken as required.' Since there were several dozen pellets left, his mother-in-law must have died before developing an opium habit. A merciful release, he reflected, popping the bottle into the pocket of his houndstooth jacket. It would have been too tiresome if she had been an opium addict on top of everything else.

David poured his coffee into a thin round eighteenth-century china cup, decorated with gold and orange cockerels fighting one another under a gold and orange tree. He took the bottle from his pocket, shook three white pellets into his hand and swallowed them with a gulp of coffee. Excited by the idea of resting comfortably under the influence of opium, he celebrated with some brandy made in the year of his birth, a present to himself which, as he told Eleanor when she paid for a case of it, reconciled him to growing old. To complete the portrait of his contentment he lit a cigar and sat in a deep chair beside the window with a battered copy of Surtees's *Jorrocks' Jaunts and Jollities*. He read the first sentence with familiar pleasure, 'What truebred city sportsman has not in his day put off the most urgent business – perhaps his marriage, or even the interment of his rib – that he might "Brave the morn" with that renowned pack, the Surrey Subscription Fox Hounds?'

When David woke up a couple of hours later, he felt tied down to a turbulent sleep by thousands of small elastic strings. He looked up slowly from the ridges and the valleys of his trousers and focused on his coffee cup. It seemed to have a thin luminous band around its edges and to be slightly raised above the surface of the small round table it lay on. He was disturbed but fascinated when he noticed that one of the gold and orange cockerels was very slowly pecking out the eye of the other. He had not expected to hallucinate. Although extraordinarily free from pain, he was worried by the loss of control that hallucination entailed.

The armchair felt like a cheese fondue as he dragged himself out of it, and walking across the floor reminded him of climbing a sand dune. He poured two glasses of cold coffee and drank them straight down, hoping they would sober him up before Eleanor returned with Nicholas and that girl of his.

He wanted to go for a brisk walk, but could not help stopping to admire the luxurious glow of his surroundings. He became particularly engrossed in the black Chinese cabinet and the colourful figures embossed on its lacquered surface. The palanquin in which an important mandarin lounged shifted forward, and the parasol held above his head by servants in shallow straw hats started to revolve hesitatingly.

David tore himself away from this animated scene and went outside. Before he could find out whether fresh air would dispel his nausea and give him back the control he wanted, he heard the sound of Eleanor's car coming down the drive. He doubled back, grabbed his copy of Surtees, and retreated into the library.

After Anne had been dropped off at Victor's, Nicholas took her place in the front passenger seat. Bridget sprawled in the back sleepily. Eleanor and Nicholas had been talking about people she didn't know.

'I'd almost forgotten how wonderful it is here,' said Nicholas, as they approached the house.

'I've completely forgotten,' said Eleanor, 'and I live here.'

'Oh, Eleanor, what a sad thing to say,' said Nicholas. 'Tell me it isn't true quickly, or I won't enjoy my tea.'

'OK,' said Eleanor, lowering the electric window to flick a cigarette out, 'it isn't true.'

'Good girl,' said Nicholas.

Bridget couldn't think of anything to say about her

new surroundings. Through the car window she could see wide steps sweeping down beside a large house with pale blue shutters. Wisteria and honeysuckle climbed and tumbled at various points along the side of the house to break the monotony of the stone. She felt she had seen it all before, and for her it had only the slim reality of a photograph in the flicked pages of a magazine. The dope had made her feel sexy. She was longing to masturbate and felt remote from the chatter going on around her.

'François should come to fetch your bags,' said Eleanor. 'Leave them in the car and he'll bring them later.'

'Oh, it's all right, I can manage the bags,' said Nicholas. He wanted to get Bridget alone in their room for a moment and tell her to 'buck up'.

'No, really, let François do it, he's had nothing to do all day,' said Eleanor, who didn't want to be left alone with David.

Nicholas had to content himself with beaming his unspoken disapproval towards Bridget, who wandered down the steps trying to avoid the cracks between the paving stones, and did not even glance in his direction.

When they arrived in the hall, Eleanor was delighted by David's absence. Perhaps he had drowned in the bath. It was too much to hope. She sent Nicholas and Bridget out onto the terrace and went to the kitchen to ask Yvette for some tea. On the way she drank a glass of brandy.

'Could you bear to make a little light conversation now and again?' said Nicholas as soon as he was alone with Bridget. 'You haven't yet addressed a word to Eleanor.'

'OK, darling,' said Bridget, still trying not to walk on the cracks. She turned towards Nicholas and said in a loud whisper, 'Is this the one?'

'What?'

'The fig tree where he made her eat on all fours.'

Nicholas looked up at the windows above him, remembering the conversations he had overheard from his bedroom the last time he was staying. He nodded, putting his fingers to his lips.

Figs littered the ground underneath the tree. Some were reduced to a black stain and a few pips, but a number had not yet decayed and their purple skins, covered in a dusty white film, were still unbroken. Bridget knelt down like a dog on the ground.

'For God's sake,' snarled Nicholas, leaping over to her side. At that moment the drawing room door opened and Yvette came out, carrying a tray of cakes and cups. She only glimpsed what was going on, but it confirmed her suspicion that rich English people had a strange relationship with the animal kingdom. Bridget rose, smirking.

'*Ah, fantastique de vous revoir, Yvette,*' said Nicholas.

'*Bonjour, Monsieur.*'

'*Bonjour,*' said Bridget prettily.

'*Bonjour, Madame,*' said Yvette stoutly, though she knew that Bridget was not married.

'David!' roared Nicholas over Yvette's head. 'Where have you been hiding?'

David waved his cigar at Nicholas. 'Got lost in Surtees,' he said, stepping through the doorway. He wore his dark glasses to protect him from surprises. 'Hello, my dear,' he said to Bridget, whose name he had forgotten. 'Have either of you seen Eleanor? I caught a glimpse of some pink trousers rounding a corner, but they didn't answer to her name.'

'That's certainly what she was last seen wearing,' said Nicholas.

'Pink suits her so well, don't you think?' said David to Bridget. 'It matches the colour of her eyes.'

'Wouldn't some tea be delicious?' said Nicholas quickly.

Bridget poured the tea, while David went to sit on a

low wall, a few feet away from Nicholas. As he tapped his cigar gently and let the ash fall at his feet, he noticed a trail of ants working their way along the side of the wall and into their nest in the corner.

Bridget carried cups of tea over to the two men, and as she turned to fetch her own cup, David held the burning tip of his cigar close to the ants and ran it along in both directions as far as he could conveniently reach. The ants twisted, excruciated by the heat, and dropped down onto the terrace. Some, before they fell, reared up, their stitching legs trying helplessly to repair their ruined bodies.

'What a civilized life you have here,' Bridget sang out as she sank back into a dark-blue deckchair. Nicholas rolled his eyeballs and wondered why the hell he had told her to make light conversation. To cover the silence he remarked to David that he had been to Jonathan Croyden's memorial service the day before.

'Do you find that you go to more memorial services, or more weddings these days?' David asked.

'I still get more wedding invitations, but I find I enjoy the memorials more.'

'Because you don't have to bring a present?'

'Well, that helps a great deal, but mainly because one

gets a better crowd when someone really distinguished dies.'

'Unless all his friends have died before him.'

'That, of course, is intolerable,' said Nicholas categorically.

'Ruins the party.'

'Absolutely.'

'I'm afraid I don't approve of memorial services,' said David, taking another puff on his cigar. 'Not merely because I cannot imagine anything in most men's lives that deserves to be celebrated, but also because the delay between the funeral and the memorial service is usually so long that, far from rekindling the spirit of a lost friend, it only shows how easily one can live without him.' David blew on the tip of his cigar and it glowed brightly. The opium made him feel that he was listening to another man speak.

'The dead are dead,' he went on, 'and the truth is that one forgets about people when they stop coming to dinner. There are exceptions, of course – namely, the people one forgets *during* dinner.'

With his cigar he caught a stray ant which was escaping with singed antennae from his last incendiary raid. 'If you really miss someone, you are better off doing something you both enjoyed doing together, which is unlikely to mean, except in the most bizarre cases, standing around in a draughty church, wearing a black overcoat and singing hymns.'

The ant ran away with astonishing speed and was about to reach the far side of the wall when David, stretching a little, touched it lightly with a surgeon's precision. Its skin blistered and it squirmed violently as it died.

'One should only go to an enemy's memorial service. Quite apart from the pleasure of outlasting him, it is an opportunity for a truce. Forgiveness is so important, don't you think?'

'Gosh, yes,' said Bridget, 'especially getting other people to forgive you.'

David smiled at her encouragingly, until he saw Eleanor step through the doorway.

'Ah, Eleanor,' grinned Nicholas with exaggerated pleasure, 'we were just talking about Jonathan Croyden's memorial.'

'I guess it's the end of an era,' said Eleanor.

'He *was* the last man alive to have gone to one of Evelyn Waugh's parties in drag,' said Nicholas. 'He was said to dress much better as a woman than as a man. He was an inspiration to a whole generation of Englishmen. Which reminds me, after the memorial I met a very tiresome, smarmy Indian who claimed to have visited you just before staying with Jonathan at Cap Ferrat.'

'It must have been Vijay,' said Eleanor. 'Victor brought him over.'

'That's the one,' Nicholas nodded. 'He seemed to know that I was coming here. Perfectly extraordinary as I'd never set eyes on him before.'

'He's desperately fashionable,' explained David, 'and consequently knows more about people he has never met than he does about anything else.'

Eleanor perched on a frail white chair with a faded blue cushion on its circular seat. She rose again immediately and dragged the chair further towards the shade of the fig tree.

'Watch out,' said Bridget, 'you might squash some of the figs.'

Eleanor made no reply.

'It seems a pity to waste them,' said Bridget innocently, leaning over to pick a fig off the ground. 'This one is perfect.' She brought it close to her mouth. 'Isn't it weird the way their skin is purple and white at the same time.'

'Like a drunk with emphysema,' said David, smiling at Eleanor.

Bridget opened her mouth, rounded her lips and pushed the fig inside. She suddenly felt what she later described to Barry as a 'very heavy vibe' from David, 'as if he was pushing his fist into my womb'. Bridget swallowed the fig, but she felt a physical need to get out of the deckchair and move further away from David.

She walked beside the edge of the wall above the garden terrace and, wanting to explain her sudden action, she stretched out her arms, embraced the view, and said, 'What a perfect day.' Nobody replied. Scanning the landscape for something else to say, she glimpsed a slight movement at the far end of the garden. At first she thought it was an animal crouched under the pear tree, but when it got up she saw that it was a child. 'Is that your son?' she asked. 'In the red trousers.'

Eleanor walked over to her side. 'Yes, it's Patrick. Patrick!' she shouted. 'Do you want some tea, darling?'

There was no answer. 'Maybe he can't hear you,' said Bridget.

'Of course he can,' said David. 'He's just being tiresome.'

'Maybe we can't hear him,' said Eleanor. 'Patrick!' she shouted again. 'Why don't you come and have some tea with us?'

'He's shaking his head,' said Bridget.

'He's probably had tea two or three times already,' said Nicholas; 'you know what they're like at that age.'

'God, children are so *sweet*,' said Bridget, smiling at Eleanor. 'Eleanor,' she said in the same tone, as if her request should be granted as a reward for finding children sweet, 'could you tell me which room I'm in because I'd quite like to go up and have a bath and unpack.'

'Of course. Let me show you,' said Eleanor.

Eleanor led Bridget into the house.

'Your girlfriend is very, I believe the word is "vivacious",' said David.

'Oh, she'll do for now,' said Nicholas.

'No need to apologize, she's absolutely charming. Shall we have a real drink?'

'Good idea.'

'Champagne?'

'Perfect.'

David fetched the champagne and reappeared tearing the golden lead from the neck of a clear bottle.

'Cristal,' said Nicholas dutifully.

'Nothing but the best, or go without,' said David.

'It reminds me of Charles Pewsey,' said Nicholas. 'We were drinking a bottle of that stuff at Wilton's last week and I asked him if he remembered Gunter,

Jonathan Croyden's unspeakable amanuensis. And Charles roared – you know how deaf he is – "Amanuensis? Bumboy, you mean: *unspeakable bumboy*." Everyone turned round and stared at us.'

'They always do when one's with Charles.' David grinned. It was so typical of Charles, one had to know Charles to appreciate how funny it was.

The bedroom Bridget had been put in was all flowery chintz, with engravings of Roman ruins on every wall. Beside the bed was a copy of Lady Mosley's *A Life of Contrasts*, on top of which Bridget had thrown *Valley of the Dolls*, her current reading. She sat by the window smoking a joint, and watched the smoke drift through the tiny holes in the mosquito net. From below, she could hear Nicholas shout *'unspeakable bumboy'*. They must be reminiscing about their school days. Boys will be boys.

Bridget lifted one foot onto the windowsill. She still held the joint in her left hand, although it would burn her fingers with the next toke. She slipped her right hand between her legs and started to masturbate.

'It just goes to show that being an amanuensis doesn't matter as long as you have the butler on your side,' said Nicholas.

David picked up his cue. 'It's always the same thing

in life,' he chanted. 'It's not what you do, it's who you know.'

To find such a ludicrous example of this important maxim made the two men laugh.

Bridget moved over to the bed and spread herself out face down on the yellow bedcover. As she closed her eyes and resumed masturbating, the thought of David flashed over her like a static shock, but she forced herself to focus loyally on the memory of Barry's stirring presence.

9

When Victor was in trouble with his writing he had a nervous habit of flicking open his pocket watch and clicking it closed again. Distracted by the noise of other human activities he found it helpful to make a noise of his own. During the contemplative passages of his daydreams he flicked and clicked more slowly, but as he pressed up against his sense of frustration the pace increased.

Dressed this morning in the flecked and bulky sweater he had hunted down ruthlessly for an occasion on which clothes simply didn't matter, he fully intended to begin his essay on the necessary and sufficient conditions of personal identity. He sat at a slightly wobbly wooden table under a yellowing plane tree in front of the house, and as the temperature rose he stripped down to his shirtsleeves. By lunchtime he had recorded only one thought, 'I have written books which I have had to write, but I have not yet written a book which others have to read.' He punished himself by improvising a sandwich for lunch, instead of walking down to La Coquière and eating three courses in the garden, under the blue and red and yellow parasol of the Ricard Pastis company.

Despite himself he kept thinking of Eleanor's puzzled little contribution that morning, 'Gosh, I mean, if anything is in the mind, it's who you are.' If anything is in the mind it's who you are: it was silly, it was unhelpful, but it whined about him like a mosquito in the dark.

Just as a novelist may sometimes wonder why he invents characters who do not exist and makes them do things which do not matter, so a philosopher may wonder why he invents cases that cannot occur in order to determine what must be the case. After a long neglect of his subject, Victor was not as thoroughly convinced that impossibility was the best route to necessity as he might have been had he recently reconsidered Stolkin's extreme case in which 'scientists destroy my brain and body, and then make out of new matter, a replica of Greta Garbo'. How could one help agreeing with Stolkin that 'there would be no connection between me and the resulting person'?

Nevertheless, to think one knew what would happen to a person's sense of identity if his brain was cut in half and distributed between identical twins seemed, just for now, before he had thrown himself back into the torrent of philosophical debate, a poor substitute for an intelligent description of what it is to know who you are.

Victor went indoors to fetch the familiar tube of Bisodol indigestion tablets. As usual he had eaten his sandwich too fast, pushing it down his throat like a sword-swallower. He thought with renewed appreciation of William James's remark that the self consists mainly of 'peculiar motions in the head and between the head and throat', although the peculiar motions somewhat lower down in his stomach and bowels felt at least as personal.

When Victor sat down again he pictured himself thinking, and tried to superimpose this picture on his inner vacancy. If he was essentially a thinking machine, then he needed to be serviced. It was not the problems of philosophy but the problem *with* philosophy that preoccupied him that afternoon. And yet how often the two became indistinguishable. Wittgenstein had said that the philosopher's treatment of a question was like the treatment of a disease. But which treatment?

Purging? Leeches? Antibiotics against the infections of language? Indigestion tablets, thought Victor, belching softly, to help break down the doughy bulk of sensation?

We ascribe thoughts to thinkers because this is the way we speak, but persons need not be claimed to be the thinkers of these thoughts. Still, thought Victor lazily, why not bow down to popular demand on this occasion? As to brains and minds, was there really any problem about two categorically different phenomena, brain process and consciousness, occurring simultaneously? Or was the problem with the categories?

From down the hill Victor heard a car door slam. It must be Eleanor dropping Anne at the bottom of the drive. Victor flicked open his watch, checked the time, and snapped it closed again. What had he achieved? Almost nothing. It was not one of those unproductive days when he was confused by abundance and starved, like Buridan's ass, between two equally nourishing bales of hay. His lack of progress today was more profound.

He watched Anne rounding the last corner of the drive, painfully bright in her white dress.

'Hi,' she said.

'Hello,' said Victor with boyish gloom.

'How's it going?'

'Oh, it's been a fairly futile exercise, but I suppose it's good to get any exercise at all.'

'Don't knock that futile exercise,' said Anne, 'it's big business. Bicycles that don't go anyplace, a long walk to nowhere on a rubber treadmill, heavy things you don't even *need* to pick up.'

Victor remained silent, staring down at his one sentence. Anne rested her hands on his shoulders. 'So there's no major news on who we are?'

'Afraid not. Personal identity, of course, is a fiction, a pure fiction. But I've reached this conclusion by the wrong method.'

'What was that?'

'Not thinking about it.'

'But that's what the English mean, isn't it, when they say, "He was very philosophical about it"? They mean that someone stopped thinking about something.' Anne lit a cigarette.

'Still,' said Victor in a quiet voice, 'my thinking today reminds me of a belligerent undergraduate I once taught, who said that our tutorials had "failed to pass the So What Test".'

Anne sat down on the edge of Victor's table and eased off one of her canvas shoes with the toe of the other. She liked to see Victor working again, however unsuccessfully. Placing her bare foot on his knee, she said, 'Tell me, Professor, is this *my* foot?'

'Well, some philosophers would say that under certain circumstances,' said Victor, lifting her foot in his cupped hands, 'this would be determined by whether the foot is in pain.'

'What's wrong with the foot being in pleasure?'

'Well,' said Victor, solemnly considering this absurd question, 'in philosophy as in life, pleasure is more likely to be an hallucination. Pain is the key to possession.' He opened his mouth wide, like a hungry man approaching a hamburger, but closed it again, and gently kissed each toe.

Victor released her foot and Anne kicked off the other shoe. 'I'll be back in a moment,' she said, walking out carefully over the warm sharp gravel to the kitchen door.

Victor reflected with satisfaction that in ancient Chinese society the little game he had played with Anne's foot would have been considered almost intolerably familiar. An unbound foot represented for the Chinese a degree of abandon which genitals could never achieve. He was stimulated by the thought of how intense his desire would have been at another time, in another place. He thought of the lines from *The Jew of Malta*, 'Thou hast committed Fornication: but that was in another country, and besides the wench is dead.' In the past he had been a Utilitarian seducer, aiming to increase the sum of *general* pleasure, but since starting his affair with Anne he had been unprecedentedly faithful. Never physically alluring, he had always relied on his cleverness to seduce women. As he grew uglier and more famous, so the instrument of seduction, his speech, and the instrument of gratification, his body, grew into an increasingly inglorious contrast. The routine of fresh seductions highlighted this aspect of the mind–body problem more harshly than intimacy, and he had decided that perhaps it was time to be in the same country with a living wench. The challenge was not to substitute a mental absence for a physical one.

Anne came out of the house carrying two glasses of orange juice. She gave one to Victor.

'What were you thinking?' she asked.

'Whether you would be the same person in another body,' lied Victor.

'Well, ask yourself, would you be nibbling my toes if I looked like a Canadian lumberjack?'

'If I knew it was *you* inside,' said Victor loyally.

'Inside the steel-capped boots?'

'Exactly.'

They smiled at each other. Victor took a gulp of orange juice. 'But tell me,' he said, 'how was your expedition with Eleanor?'

'On the way back I found myself thinking that everybody who is meeting for dinner tonight will probably have said something unkind about everybody else. I know you'll think it's very primitive and American of me, but why do people spend the evening with people they've spent the day insulting?'

'So as to have something insulting to say about them tomorrow.'

'Why, of course,' gasped Anne. '*Tomorrow is another day*. So different and yet so similar,' she added.

Victor looked uneasy. 'Were you insulting each other in the car, or just attacking David and me?'

'Neither, but the way that everyone else was insulted I knew that we would break off into smaller and smaller combinations, until everyone had been dealt with by everyone else.'

'But that's what charm is: being malicious about everybody except the person you are with, who then glows with the privilege of exemption.'

'If that's what charm is,' said Anne, 'it broke down

on this occasion, because I felt that none of us was exempt.'

'Do you wish to confirm your own theory by saying something nasty about one of your fellow dinner guests?'

'Well, now that you mention it,' said Anne, laughing, 'I thought that Nicholas Pratt was a total creep.'

'I know what you mean. His problem is that he wanted to go into politics,' Victor explained, 'but was destroyed by what passed for a sex scandal some years ago and would probably now be called an "open marriage". Most people wait until they've become ministers to ruin their political careers with a sex scandal, but Nicholas managed to do it when he was still trying to impress Central Office by contesting a by-election in a safe Labour seat.'

'Precocious, huh,' said Anne. 'What exactly did he do to deserve his exile from paradise?'

'He was found in bed with two women he was not married to by the woman he was married to, and she decided not to "stand by his side".'

'Sounds like there wasn't any room,' said Anne, 'but like you say, it was bad timing. Back in those days you couldn't go on television and say how it was a "really liberating experience".'

'There may still be,' said Victor with mock astonishment, joining the tips of his fingers pedagogically, to form an arc with his hands, 'certain rural backwaters of Tory England where, even today, group sex is not practised by *all* the matrons on the Selection Committee.'

Anne sat down on Victor's knee. 'Victor, do two people make a group?'

'Only part of a group, I'm afraid.'

'You mean,' said Anne with horror, 'we've been having part-of-a-group sex?' She got up again, ruffling Victor's hair. 'That's awful.'

'I think,' Victor continued calmly, 'that when his political ambitions were ruined so early, Nicholas became rather indifferent to a career and fell back on his large inheritance.'

'He still doesn't make it on to my casualty list,' said Anne. 'Being found in bed with two girls isn't the shower room in Auschwitz.'

'You have high standards.'

'I do and I don't. No pain is too small if it hurts, but any pain is too small if it's cherished,' Anne said. 'Anyhow, he isn't suffering that badly, he's got a stoned schoolgirl with him. She was being moody in the back of the car. Two like her isn't enough, he'll have to graduate to triplets.'

'What's she called?'

'Bridget something. One of those not very convincing English names like Hop-Scotch.'

Anne moved on quickly, she was determined not to let Victor get lost in ruminations about where Bridget might 'fit in'. 'The oddest thing about the day was our visit to Le Wild Ouest.'

'Why on earth did you go there?'

'As far as I could make out we were there because Patrick wants to go, but Eleanor gets priority.'

'You don't think she might have just been checking whether it was an amusing place to take her son?'

'In the Dodge City of arrested development, you gotta be quick on the draw,' said Anne, whipping out an imaginary gun.

'You seem to have entered into the spirit of the place,' said Victor drily.

'If she wanted to take her son there,' Anne resumed, 'he could have come with us. And if she wanted to find out whether it was an "amusing place", Patrick could have told her.'

Victor did not want to argue with Anne. She often had strong opinions about human situations which did not really matter to him, unless they illustrated a principle or yielded an anecdote, and he preferred to concede this stony ground to her, with whatever show of leniency his mood required. 'There isn't anyone at dinner tonight left for us to disparage,' he said, 'except David, and we know what you think of him.'

'That reminds me, I must read at least a chapter of *The Twelve Caesars* so I can give it back to him this evening.'

'Read the chapters on Nero and Caligula,' Victor suggested, 'I'm sure they're David's favourites. One illustrates what happens when you combine a mediocre artistic talent with absolute power. The other shows how nearly inevitable it is for those who have been terrified to become terrifying, once they have the opportunity.'

'But isn't that the key to a great education? You spend your adolescence being promoted from terrified to terrifier, without any women around to distract you.'

Victor decided to ignore this latest demonstration of Anne's rather tiresome attitude towards English public schools. 'The interesting thing about Caligula,' he went on patiently, 'is that he intended to be a model emperor, and for the first few months of his reign he was praised for his magnanimity. But the compulsion to repeat what one has experienced is like gravity, and it takes special equipment to break away from it.'

Anne was amused to hear Victor make such an overtly psychological generalization. Perhaps if people had been dead long enough they came alive for him.

'Nero I dislike for having driven Seneca to suicide,' Victor droned on. 'Although I'm well aware of the hostility that can arise between a pupil and his tutor, it is just as well to keep it within limits,' he chuckled.

'Didn't Nero commit suicide himself, or was that just in *Nero, the Movie*?'

'When it came to suicide he showed less enthusiasm than he had done for driving other people to it. He sat around for a long time wondering which part of his "pustular and malodorous" body to puncture, wailing, "Dead and so great an artist!"'

'You sound like you were there.'

'You know how it is with the books one reads in one's youth.'

'Yeah, that's kinda how I feel about *Francis the Talking Mule*,' said Anne.

She got up from the creaking wicker chair. 'I guess I'd better catch up on "one's youth" before dinner.' She moved over to Victor's side. 'Write me one sentence before we have to go,' she said gently. 'You can do that, can't you?'

Victor enjoyed being coaxed. He looked up at her like an obedient child. 'I'll try,' he said modestly.

Anne walked through the gloom of the kitchen and climbed the twisting stairs. She felt a cool pleasure at being alone for the first time since the early morning and wanted to have a bath straight away. Victor liked to wallow in the tub, controlling the taps with his big toe, and she knew how irrationally disappointed he became if the steaming water ran out during this important ceremony. Besides, if she bathed now she could lie on her bed and read for a couple of hours before going out to dinner.

On top of the books by her bed was *Goodbye to Berlin* and Anne thought how much more fun it would be to reread that rather than dip into the grisly Caesars. From the thought of pre-war Berlin her mind jumped back to the remark she had made about the shower room in Auschwitz. Was she, she wondered, giving in to that English need to be facetious? She felt tainted and exhausted by a summer of burning up her moral resources for the sake of small conversational effects. She felt she had been subtly perverted by slick and lazy English manners, the craving for the prophylactic of irony, the terrible fear of being 'a bore', and the boredom of the ways they relentlessly and narrowly evaded this fate.

Above all it was Victor's ambivalence towards these values that was wearing her down. She could no longer tell whether he was working as a double agent, a serious writer pretending to the Folks on the Hill – of which the Melroses were only rather a tarnished example – that he was a devoted admirer of the effortless nullity of their lives. Or perhaps he was a triple agent, pretending to her that he had not accepted the bribe of being admitted to the periphery of their world.

Defiantly, Anne picked up *Goodbye to Berlin* and headed towards the bathroom.

The sun disappeared early behind the roof of the tall, narrow house. At his table under the plane tree Victor put his sweater back on. He felt safe in the bulk of his sweater with the distant sound of Anne running her bath. He wrote a sentence in his spidery hand, and then another.

10

If David had awarded himself the most important painting in the house, at least Eleanor had secured the largest bedroom. At the far end of the corridor, its curtains were closed all day to protect a host of frail Italian drawings from the draining power of the sun.

Patrick hesitated in the doorway of his mother's bedroom, waiting to be noticed. The dimness of the room made it seem even larger, especially when a breeze stirred the curtains and an unsteady light spread shadows over the stretching walls. Eleanor sat at her desk with her back to Patrick, writing a cheque to the Save the Children Fund, her favourite charity. She did not hear her son come into the room until he stood beside her chair.

'Hello, darling,' she said, with a desperate affection

that sounded like a long-distance telephone call. 'What did you do today?'

'Nothing,' said Patrick, looking down at the floor.

'Did you go for a walk with Daddy?' asked Eleanor bravely. She felt the inadequacy of her questions, but could not overcome the dread of having them scantily answered.

Patrick shook his head. A branch swayed outside the window, and he watched the shadow of its leaves flickering above the curtain pole. The curtains billowed feebly and collapsed again, like defeated lungs. Down the corridor a door slammed. Patrick looked at the clutter on his mother's desk. It was covered in letters, envelopes, paper clips, rubber bands, pencils, and a profusion of different-coloured chequebooks. An empty champagne glass stood beside a full ashtray.

'Shall I take the glass down?' he asked.

'What a thoughtful boy you are,' gushed Eleanor. 'You could take it down and give it to Yvette. That would be very kind.'

Patrick nodded solemnly and picked up the glass. Eleanor marvelled at how well her son had turned out. Perhaps people were just born one way or another and the main thing was not to interfere too much.

'Thank you, darling,' she said huskily, wondering

what she was meant to have done, as she watched him walk out of the room, gripping the stem of the glass tightly in his right hand.

As Patrick was going down the staircase, he overheard his father and Nicholas talking at the other end of the corridor. Suddenly afraid of falling, he started to walk down the way he used to when he was little, leading with one foot, and then bringing the other down firmly beside it on the same step. He had to hurry in case his father caught up with him, but if he hurried he might fall. He heard his father saying, 'We'll put it to him at dinner, I'm sure he'll agree.'

Patrick froze on the stairs. They were talking about him. They were going to make him agree. Squeezing the stem of the glass fiercely in his hand, he felt a rush of shame and terror. He looked up at the painting hanging on the stairs and imagined its frame hurtling through the air and embedding its sharp corner in his father's chest; and another painting whistling down the corridor and chopping Nicholas's head off.

'I'll see you downstairs in an hour or two,' said Nicholas.

'Right-ho,' said his father.

Patrick heard Nicholas's door close, and he listened intently to his father's footsteps coming down the corridor. Was he going to his bedroom, or coming down the stairs? Patrick wanted to move, but the power to move had deserted him again. He held his breath as the footsteps stopped.

In the corridor David was torn between visiting Eleanor, with whom he was always furious on principle, and going to have a bath. The opium which had taken the edge off the perpetual ache in his body now weakened his desire to insult his wife. After a few moments spent considering the choice he went into his bedroom.

Patrick knew he was not visible from the top of the stairs, but when he heard the footsteps pause he had tried to push back the idea of his father with concentration like a flamethrower. For a long time after David had gone into his bedroom, Patrick did not accept that the danger was over. When he relaxed his grip on the glass, the base and half the stem slipped out of his hand and broke on the step below him. Patrick couldn't understand how the glass had snapped. Removing the rest of the glass from his hand, he saw a small cut in the middle of his palm. Only when he saw it bleed did he understand what had happened and, knowing that he must be in pain, he at last felt the sharp sting of the cut.

He was terrified of being punished for dropping the

glass. It had fallen apart in his hand, but they would never believe that, they would say that he'd dropped it. He stepped carefully among the scattered pieces of glass on the steps below and got to the bottom of the stairs, but he did not know what to do with the half glass in his hand, and so he climbed back up three of the steps and decided to jump. He threw himself forward as hard as he could, but tripped as he landed, letting the rest of the glass fly from his hand and shatter against the wall. He lay splayed and shocked on the floor.

When she heard Patrick's screams, Yvette put down the soup ladle, wiped her hands quickly on her apron, and hurried into the hall.

'*Ooh-la-la*,' she said reproachfully, '*tu vas te casser la figure un de ces jours.*' She was alarmed by Patrick's helplessness, but as she drew closer she asked him more gently, '*Où est-ce que ça te fait mal, pauvre petit?*'

Patrick still felt the shock of being winded and pointed to his chest where he had taken the brunt of the fall. Yvette picked him up, murmuring, '*Allez, c'est pas grave*,' and kissed him on the cheek. He went on crying, but less desperately. A tangled sensation of sweat and gold teeth and garlic mingled with the pleasure of being held, but when Yvette started to rub his back, he squirmed in her arms and broke free.

At her desk Eleanor thought, 'Oh God, he's fallen downstairs and cut himself on the glass I gave him. It's my fault again.' Patrick's screaming impaled her on her chair like a javelin, while she considered the horror of her position.

Still dominated by guilt and the fear of David's reprisals, she summoned up the courage to go out onto the landing. At the bottom of the stairs she found Yvette sitting beside Patrick.

'*Rien de cassé, Madame,*' said Yvette. '*Il a eu peur en tombant, c'est tout.*'

'*Merci, Yvette,*' said Eleanor.

It wasn't practical to drink as much as she did, thought Yvette, going to fetch a dustpan and brush.

Eleanor sat down beside Patrick, but a fragment of glass cut into her bottom. 'Ouch,' she exclaimed, and got up again to brush the back of her dress.

'Mummy sat on a piece of glass,' she said to Patrick. He looked at her glumly. 'But never mind about that, tell me about your terrible fall.'

'I jumped down from very high up.'

'With a glass in your hand, darling? That could have been very dangerous.'

'It was dangerous,' said Patrick angrily.

'Oh, I'm sure it was,' said Eleanor, reaching out self-consciously to brush back the fringe of light brown hair from his forehead. 'I'll tell you what we could do,' she said, proud of herself for remembering, 'we could go to the funfair tomorrow, to Le Wild Ouest, would you like that? I went there today with Anne to see if you would like it, and there were lots of cowboys and Indians and rides. Shall we go tomorrow?'

'I want to go away,' said Patrick.

Up in his monk's suite, David hurried next door and turned the bath taps to their full volume, until the thundering water drowned the uncongenial sound of his son. He sprinkled bath salts into the water from a porcelain shell and thought how intolerable it was having no nanny this summer to keep the boy quiet in the evenings. Eleanor hadn't the least idea of how to bring up a child.

After Patrick's nanny had died, there had been a dim procession of foreign girls through the London house. Homesick vandals, they left in tears after a few months, sometimes pregnant, never any more fluent in the English they had come to learn. In the end Patrick was often entrusted to Carmen, the morose Spanish maid who could not be bothered to refuse him anything. She lived in the basement, her varicose veins protesting at every step of the five storeys she seldom climbed to the nursery. In a sense one had to be grateful that this lugubrious peasant had had so little influence on Patrick. Still, it was very tiresome to find him on the stairs night after night, escaped from behind his wooden gate, waiting for Eleanor.

They so often returned late from Annabel's that Patrick had once asked anxiously, 'Who is Annabels?' Everyone in the room had laughed and David could remember Bunny Warren saying, with that simple-hearted tactlessness for which he was almost universally adored, 'She's a very lovely young girl your parents are exceptionally fond of.' Nicholas had seen his chance and said, 'I sospect ze child is experienzing ze sibling rivalry.'

When David came in late at night and found Patrick sitting on the stairs, he would order him back to the nursery, but after he had gone to bed he sometimes heard the floorboards creak on the landing. He knew that Patrick crept into his mother's room to try to extract some consolation from her stupefied back, as she lay curled up and unconscious on the edge of her mattress. He had seen them in the morning like refugees in an expensive waiting room.

David turned off the taps and found that the screaming had stopped. Screaming that only lasted as long as it took to fill a bath could not be taken seriously. David tested the water with a foot. It was far too hot, but he pushed his leg down deeper until the water covered his hairless shin, and started to scald him. Every nerve in his body urged him to step out of the steaming bath, but he called up his deep resources of contempt and kept his leg immersed to prove his mastery over the pain.

He straddled the bath; one foot burning, the other cool against the cork floor. It took no effort for him to revive the fury he had felt an hour earlier when he glimpsed Bridget kneeling under the tree. Nicholas had obviously told that silly bitch about the figs.

Oh, happy days, he sighed, where had they fled? Days when his now bedraggled wife, still freshly submissive and eager to please, had grazed so peacefully among the rotting figs.

David hoisted his other leg over the side of the bath and plunged it into the water, in the hope that the additional pain would stimulate him to think of the right revenge to take on Nicholas during dinner.

'Why the hell did you have to do that? I'm sure David saw you,' Nicholas snapped at Bridget, as soon as he had heard David's bedroom door close.

'Saw what?'

'You, down on all fours.'

'I didn't have to,' said Bridget sleepily from the bed. 'I only did it because you were so keen to tell me the story, and I thought it might turn you on. It obviously did the first time.'

'Don't be so absurd.' Nicholas stood with his hands on his hips, a picture of disapproval. 'As to your effusive remarks – "What a perfect life you have here",' he simpered, ' "What a wonderful view" – they made you sound even more vulgar and stupid than you are.'

Bridget still had trouble in taking Nicholas's rudeness seriously.

'If you're going to be horrid,' she said, 'I'll elope with Barry.'

'And that's another thing,' gasped Nicholas, removing his silk jacket. There were dark sweat rings under the arms of his shirt. 'What was going through your mind – if mind is the right word – when you gave that yob the telephone number here?'

'When I said that we must keep in touch, he asked me for the number of the house I was staying in.'

'You could have lied, you know,' yelped Nicholas. 'There's such a thing as dishonesty.' He paced up and down shaking his head. 'Such a thing as a broken promise.'

Bridget rolled off the bed and crossed the room. 'Just fuck off,' she said, slamming the bathroom door and locking it. She sat on the edge of the bath and remembered that her copy of *Tatler* and, worse, her make-up were in the room next door.

'Open the door, you stupid bitch,' said Nicholas swivelling the doorknob.

'Fuck off,' she repeated. At least she could prevent Nicholas from using the bathroom for as long as possible, even if she only had a bubble bath to amuse her.

11

While he was locked out of the bathroom Nicholas unpacked and filled the most convenient shelves with his shirts; in the cupboard his suits took up rather more than half the space. The biography of F. E. Smith that he had already carried with him to half a dozen houses that summer was placed again on the table on the right-hand side of the bed. When he was finally allowed access to the bathroom, he distributed his possessions around the basin in a familiar order, his badger brush to one side and his rose mouthwash to the other.

Bridget refused to unpack properly. She pulled out a frail-looking dress of dark-red crushed velvet for tonight, tossed it on the bed, and abandoned her suit-case in the middle of the floor. Nicholas could not resist kicking it over, but he said nothing, conscious that if he was rude to her again straight away she might cause him difficulties during dinner.

Silently, Nicholas put on a dark-blue silk suit and an old pale-yellow shirt, the most conventional one he had been able to find at Mr Fish, and was now ready to go downstairs. His hair smelt faintly of something made up for him by Trumper's, and his cheeks of a very simple extract of lime he considered clean and manly.

Bridget sat at the dressing table, very slowly applying too much black eyeliner.

'We must get downstairs, or we'll be late,' said Nicholas.

'You always say that and then there's nobody there.'

'David is even more punctual than I am.'

'So go down without me.'

'I would rather we went down together,' said Nicholas, with menacing weariness.

Bridget continued to admire herself in the inadequately lit mirror, while Nicholas sat on the edge of the bed and gave his shirtsleeves a little tug to reveal more of his royal cufflinks. Made of thick gold and engraved with the initials E.R., they might have been contemporary, but had in fact been a present to his rakish grandfather, the Sir Nicholas Pratt of his day and a loyal courtier of Edward VII's. Unable to think how he could further embellish his appearance, he got up and wandered around. He drifted back into the bathroom and stole another glance at himself in the mirror. The softening contours of his chin, where the flab was beginning to build up, would undoubtedly profit from yet another suntan. He dabbed a little more lime extract behind his ears.

'I'm ready,' said Bridget.

Nicholas came over to the dressing table and quickly pressed Bridget's powder puff to his cheekbones, and ran it coyly over the bridge of his nose. As they left the room, he glanced at Bridget critically, unable to approve fully of the red velvet dress he had once praised. It carried with it the aura of an antique stall in Kensington Market, and showed up its cheapness glaringly in the presence of other antiques. The red emphasized her blonde hair, and the velvet brought out the glassy blue of her eyes, but the design of the dress, which seemed to have been made for a medieval witch, and the evidence of amateur repairs in the worn material struck him as less amusing than the first time he had seen Bridget in this same dress. It had been at a half Bohemian party in Chelsea given by an ambitious Peruvian. Nicholas and the other social peaks that the host was trying to scale stood together at one end of the room insulting the mountaineer as he scrambled about them attentively. When they had nothing better to do they allowed him to bribe them with his hospitality, on the understanding he would be swept away by an avalanche of invective if he ever treated them with familiarity at a party given by people who really mattered.

Sometimes it was great festivals of privilege, and at other times it was the cringing and envy of others that confirmed one's sense of being at the top. Sometimes it was the seduction of a pretty girl that accomplished this important task and at other times it was down to one's swanky cufflinks.

'All roads lead to Rome,' murmured Nicholas complacently, but Bridget was not curious to know why.

As she had predicted, there was nobody waiting for them in the drawing room. With its curtains drawn, and lit only by pools of urine-coloured light splashed under the dark-yellow lampshades, the room looked both dim and rich. Like so many of one's friends, reflected Nicholas.

'Ah, *Extraits de Plantes Marines*,' he said, sniffing the burning essence loudly, 'you know it's impossible to get it now.' Bridget did not answer.

He moved over to the black cabinet and lifted a

bottle of Russian vodka out of a silver bucket full of ice cubes. He poured the cold viscous fluid into a small tumbler. 'They used to sell it with copper rings which sometimes overheated and spat burning essence onto the light bulbs. One evening, Monsieur et Madame de Quelque Chose were changing for dinner when the bulb in their dining room exploded, the lampshade caught fire, and the curtains burst into flames. After that, it was taken off the market.'

Bridget showed no surprise or interest. In the distance the telephone rang faintly. Eleanor so disliked the noise of telephones that there was only one in the house, at a small desk under the back stairs.

'Can I get you a drink?' asked Nicholas, knocking back his vodka in what he considered the correct Russian manner.

'Just a Coke,' said Bridget. She didn't really like alcohol, it was such a crude high. At least that was what Barry said. Nicholas opened a bottle of Coke and poured himself some more vodka, this time in a tall glass packed with ice.

There was a clicking of high heels on the tiles and Eleanor came in shyly, wearing a long purple dress.

'There's a phone call for you,' she said, smiling at

Bridget, whose name she had somehow forgotten between the telephone and the drawing room.

'Oh, wow,' said Bridget, 'for me?' She got up, making sure not to look at Nicholas. Eleanor described the route to the phone, and Bridget eventually arrived at the desk under the back stairs. 'Hello,' she said, '*hello*?' There was no answer.

By the time she returned to the drawing room Nicholas was saying, 'Well, one evening, the Marquis and Marquise de Quelque Chose were upstairs changing for a big party they were giving, when a lampshade caught fire and their drawing room was completely gutted.'

'How marvellous,' said Eleanor, with not the faintest idea of what Nicholas had been talking about. Recovering from one of those blank patches in which she could not have said what was going on around her, she knew only that there had been an interval since she was last conscious. 'Did you get through all right?' she said to Bridget.

'No. It's really weird, there was no one there. He must have run out of money.'

The phone rang again, more loudly this time through all the doors that Bridget had left open. She doubled back eagerly.

'Imagine wanting to talk to someone on the phone,' said Eleanor. 'I dread it.'

'Youth,' said Nicholas tolerantly.

'I dreaded it even more in my youth, if that's possible.'

Eleanor poured herself some whisky. She felt exhausted and restless at the same time. It was the feeling she knew better than any other. She returned to her usual seat, a low footstool wedged into the lampless corner beside the screen. As a child, when the screen had belonged to her mother, she had often squatted under its monkey-crowded branches pretending to be invisible.

Nicholas, who had been sitting tentatively on the edge of the Doge's chair, rose again nervously. 'This is David's favourite seat, isn't it?'

'I guess he won't sit in it if you're in it already,' said Eleanor.

'That's just what I'm not so sure of,' said Nicholas. 'You know how fond he is of having his own way.'

'Tell me about it,' said Eleanor flatly.

Nicholas moved to a nearby sofa and sucked another mouthful of vodka from his glass. It had taken on the taste of melted ice, which he disliked, but he rolled it around his mouth, having nothing in particular to say to Eleanor. Annoyed by Bridget's absence and apprehensive about David's arrival, he waited to see which would come through the door. He felt let down when Anne and Victor arrived first.

Anne had replaced her simple white dress with a simple black one and she already held a lighted cigarette. Victor had conquered his anxiety about what to wear and still had on the thick speckled sweater.

'Hi,' said Anne to Eleanor, and kissed her with real affection.

When the greetings were over, Nicholas could not help remarking on Victor's appearance. 'My dear chap, you look as if you're about to go mackerel fishing in the Hebrides.'

'In fact, the last time I wore this sweater,' said Victor, turning around and handing a glass to Anne, 'was when I had to see a student who was floundering badly with his D. Phil. It was called "Abelard, Nietzsche, Sade, and Beckett", which gives you some idea of the difficulties he was running into.'

Does it? thought Eleanor.

'Really, people will stop at nothing to get a doctorate these days.' Victor was warming up for the role he felt was required of him during dinner.

'But how did *your* writing go today?' asked Eleanor.

'I've been thinking all day of you taking a non-psychological approach to identity,' she lied. 'Have I got that right?'

'Absolutely,' said Victor. 'Indeed, I was so haunted by your remark, that if anything is in the mind it's who you are, that I was unable to think of anything else.'

Eleanor blushed. She felt she was being mocked. 'It sounds to me as if Eleanor is quite right,' said Nicholas gallantly. 'How can you separate who we are from who we think we are?'

'Oh, I dare say you can't,' replied Victor, 'once you have decided to consider things in that fashion. But I'm not attempting psychoanalysis, an activity, incidentally, which will seem as quaint as medieval map-making when we have an accurate picture of how the brain works.'

'Nothing a don likes more than bashing another chap's discipline,' said Nicholas, afraid that Victor was going to be a crashing bore during dinner.

'If you can call it a discipline,' chuckled Victor. 'The Unconscious, which we can only discuss when it *ceases* to be unconscious, is another medieval instrument of enquiry which enables the analyst to treat denial as evidence of its opposite. Under these rules we hang a man who denies that he is a murderer, and congratulate him if he says he is one.'

'Are you rejecting the idea that there is an unconscious?' said Anne.

'Are you rejecting the idea that there is an unconscious?' simpered Nicholas to himself in his hysterical American female voice.

'I am saying,' said Victor, 'that if we are controlled by forces we do not understand, the term for that state of affairs is ignorance. What I object to is that we turn ignorance into an inner landscape and pretend that this allegorical enterprise, which might be harmless or even charming, if it weren't so expensive and influential, amounts to a science.'

'But it helps people,' said Anne.

'Ah, the therapeutic promise,' said Victor wisely.

Standing in the doorway, David had been observing them for some time, unnoticed by anyone, except Eleanor.

'Oh, hello, David,' said Victor.

'Hi,' said Anne.

'My dear, so lovely to see you as always,' David answered, turning away from her instantly and saying to Victor, 'Do tell us more about the therapeutic promise.'

'But why don't *you* tell us?' said Victor. 'You're the doctor.'

'In my rather brief medical practice,' said David modestly, 'I found that people spend their whole lives imagining they are about to die. Their only consolation is that one day they're right. All that stands between them and this mental torture is a doctor's authority. And that is the only therapeutic promise that works.'

Nicholas was relieved to be ignored by David, whereas Anne watched with detachment the theatrical way the man set about dominating the room. Like a slave in a swamp full of bloodhounds, Eleanor longed to disappear and she cowered still closer to the screen.

David strode majestically across the room, sat in the Doge's chair and leaned towards Anne. 'Tell me, my dear,' he said, giving a little tug on the stiff silk of his dark-red trousers and crossing his legs, 'have you recovered from your quite unnecessary sacrifice, in going to the airport with Eleanor?'

'It wasn't a sacrifice, it was a pleasure,' said Anne innocently. 'And that reminds me, I've also had the pleasure of bringing back *The Twelve Caesars*. What I mean is that I had the pleasure of reading it and now you have the pleasure of getting it back.'

'So much pleasure in one day,' said David, letting one of the yellow slippers dangle from his foot.

'Right,' said Anne. 'Our cup overfloweth.'

'I've had a delightful day as well,' said David, 'there must be magic in the air.'

Nicholas glimpsed an opportunity to join the conversation without provoking David. 'So what did you think of *The Twelve Caesars*?' he asked Anne.

'Together they would have made a great jury,' said Anne, 'if you like your trials fast.' She turned her thumb towards the floor.

David let out an abrupt, 'Ha,' which showed he was amused. 'They'd have to take turns,' he said, pointing his thumbs down too.

'Absolutely,' said Anne. 'Imagine what would happen if they tried to choose a foreman.'

'And think of the Imperial Thumbache,' said David, twisting his aching thumbs up and down with childish enjoyment.

This happy vein of fantasy was interrupted by Bridget's return. After talking to Barry on the phone, Bridget had smoked another little joint and the colours around her had become very vivid. '*Love* those kinky yellow slippers,' she said to David brightly.

Nicholas winced.

'Do you really like them?' asked David, fixing her genially. 'I'm so pleased.'

David knew intuitively that Bridget would be embarrassed by discussing her phone call, but he had no time to interrogate her now because Yvette came in to announce dinner. Never mind, thought David, I can get her later. In the pursuit of knowledge, there was no point in killing the rabbit before one found out whether its eyes were allergic to shampoo, or its skin inflamed by mascara. It was ridiculous to 'break a butterfly upon a wheel'. The proper instrument for a butterfly was a pin. Stimulated by these consoling thoughts, David rose from his chair and said expansively, 'Let's have dinner.'

Disturbed by a draught from the opening door, the candles in the dining room flickered and animated the painted panels around the walls. A procession of grateful peasants, much appreciated by David, edged a little further along the twisting road that led to the castle gates, only to slip back again as the flames shifted the other way. The wheels of a cart which had been stuck in a roadside ditch, seemed to creak forward, and for a moment the donkey pulling it swelled with dark new muscles.

On the table Yvette had laid out two bowls of rouille

for the fish soup, and a sweating green bottle of Blanc de Blancs stood at either end of the table.

On the way from the drawing room to the dining room, Nicholas made one last attempt to extort some enthusiasm for his beleaguered anecdote. It now took place in the residence of the Prince et Princesse de Quelque Chose. 'Whoosh!' he shouted at Anne with an explosive gesture. 'The fifteenth-century tapestries burst into flame and their *hôtel particulier* BURNED TO THE GROUND. The reception had to be cancelled. There was a national scandal, and every bottle of Plantes Marines was banned *worldwide*.'

'As if it wasn't tough enough already being called Quelque Chose,' said Anne.

'But now you can't get it anywhere,' cried Nicholas, exhausted by his efforts.

'Sounds like the right decision. I mean, who wants their peculiar hotel burnt to the ground? Not me!'

Everyone waited to be seated and looked enquiringly at Eleanor. Although there seemed to be no room for doubt, with the women next to David and the men next to her and the couples mixed, she felt a dreadful conviction that she would make a mistake and unleash David's fury. Flustered, she stood there saying,

'Anne . . . would you . . . no, you go there . . . no, I'm sorry . . .'

'Thank God we're only six,' David said in a loud whisper to Nicholas. 'There's some chance she'll crack the problem before the soup gets cold.' Nicholas smirked obediently.

God, I hate grown-up dinner parties, thought Bridget, as Yvette brought in the steaming soup.

'Tell me, my dear, what did you make of the Emperor Galba?' said David to Anne, leaning courteously towards her, to emphasize his indifference to Bridget.

This was the line that Anne had hoped the conversation would not take. Who? she thought, but said, 'Ah, what a character! What *really* interested me, though, was the character of Caligula. Why do you think he was so obsessed with his sisters?'

'Well, you know what they say,' David grinned, 'vice is nice, but incest is best.'

'But what . . .' asked Anne, pretending to be fascinated, 'what's the psychology of a situation like that? Was it a kind of narcissism? The nearest thing to seducing himself?'

'More, I think, the conviction that only a member of his own family could have suffered as he had done. You know, of course, that Tiberius killed almost all of their relations, and so he and Drusilla were survivors of the same terror. Only she could really understand him.'

As David paused to drink some wine, Anne resumed her impersonation of an eager student. 'Something else I'd love to know is why Caligula thought that torturing his wife would reveal the reason he was so devoted to her?'

'To discover witchcraft was the official explanation, but presumably he was suspicious of affection which was divorced from the threat of death.'

'And, on a larger scale, he had the same suspicion about Roman people. Right?' asked Anne.

'Up to a point, Lord Copper,' said David. He looked as if there were things he knew, but would never divulge. So these were the benefits of a classical education, thought Anne, who had often heard David and Victor talk about them.

Victor had been eating his soup silently and very fast while Nicholas told him about Jonathan Croyden's memorial service. Eleanor had abandoned her soup and lit a cigarette; the extra Dexedrine had put her off her food. Bridget daydreamed resolutely.

'I'm afraid I don't approve of memorial services,' said Victor, pursing his lips for a moment to savour the insincerity of what he was about to say, 'they are just excuses for a party.'

'What's wrong with them,' David corrected him, 'is that they are excuses for such bad parties. I suppose you were talking about Croyden.'

'That's right,' said Victor. 'They say he spoke better than he wrote. There was certainly room for improvement.'

David bared his teeth to acknowledge this little malice. 'Did Nicholas tell you that your friend Vijay was there?'

'No,' said Victor.

'Oh,' said David, turning to Anne persuasively, 'and you never told us why he left so suddenly.' Anne had refused to answer this question on several occasions, and David liked to tease her by bringing it up whenever they met.

'Didn't I?' said Anne, playing along.

'He wasn't incontinent?' asked David.

'No,' said Anne.

'Or worse, in his case, flirtatious?'

'Absolutely not.'

'He was just being himself,' Nicholas suggested.

'That might have done it,' said Anne, 'but it was more than that.'

'The desire to pass on information is like a hunger, and sometimes it is the curiosity, sometimes the indifference, of others that arouses it,' said Victor pompously.

'OK, OK,' said Anne, to save Victor from the silence that might well follow his pronouncement. 'Now it's not going to seem like that big a deal to you sophisti-cated types,' she added demurely. 'But when I took a clean shirt of his up to his room, I found a bunch of terrible magazines. Not just pornography, much much worse. Of course I wasn't going to ask him to leave. What he reads is his own affair, but he came back and was so rude about my being in his room, when I was only there to take back his lousy shirt, that I kind of lost my temper.'

'Good for you,' said Eleanor timidly.

'What sort of magazines exactly?' asked Nicholas, sitting back and crossing his legs.

'I wish you'd confiscated them,' giggled Bridget.

'Oh, just awful,' said Anne. 'Crucifixion. All kinds of animal stuff.'

'God, how hilarious,' said Nicholas. 'Vijay rises in my estimation.'

'Oh, yeah?' said Anne. 'Well, you should have seen the look on the poor pig's face.'

Victor was a little uneasy. 'The obscure ethics of our relations to the animal kingdom,' he chuckled.

'We kill them when we feel like it,' said David crisply, 'nothing very obscure about that.'

'Ethics is not the study of what we do, my dear David, but what we ought to do,' said Victor.

'That's why it's such a waste of time, old boy,' said Nicholas cheerfully.

'Why do you think it's superior to be amoral?' Anne asked Nicholas.

'It's not a question of being superior,' he said, exposing his cavernous nostrils to Anne, 'it just springs from a desire not to be a bore or a prig.'

'Everything about Nicholas is superior,' said David, 'and even if he *were* a bore or a prig, I'm sure he would be a superior one.'

'Thank you, David,' said Nicholas with determined complacency.

'Only in the English language,' said Victor, 'can one be "a bore", like being a lawyer or a pastry cook, making boredom into a profession – in other languages a person is simply boring, a temporary state of affairs. The question is, I suppose, whether this points to a greater intolerance towards boring people, or an especially intense quality of boredom among the English.'

It's because you're such a bunch of boring old farts, thought Bridget.

Yvette took away the soup plates and closed the door behind her. The candles flickered, and the painted peasants came alive again for a moment.

'What one aims for,' said David, 'is ennui.'

'Of course,' said Anne, 'it's more than just French for our old friend boredom. It's boredom plus money, or boredom plus arrogance. It's I-find-everything-boring, therefore I'm fascinating. But it doesn't seem to occur to people that you can't have a world picture and then not be part of it.'

There was a moment of silence while Yvette came back carrying a large platter of roast veal and vegetables.

'Darling,' said David to Eleanor, 'what a marvellous memory you have to be able to duplicate the dinner you gave Anne and Victor last time they were here.'

'Oh, God, how awful,' said Eleanor. 'I'm so sorry.'

'Talking of animal ethics,' said Nicholas, 'I gather that Gerald Frogmore shot more birds last year than anyone in England. Not bad for a chap in a wheelchair.'

'Maybe he doesn't like to see things move about freely,' said Anne. She immediately felt the excitement of half wishing she had not made this remark.

'You're not anti-blood sports?' asked Nicholas, with an unspoken 'on top of everything else'.

'How could I be?' asked Anne. 'It's a middle-class prejudice based on envy. Have I got that right?'

'Well, I wasn't going to say so,' said Nicholas, 'but you put it so much better than I could possibly hope to . . .'

'Do you despise people from the middle classes?' Anne asked.

'I don't despise people *from* the middle classes, on the contrary, the further from them, the better,' said Nicholas, shooting one of his cuffs. 'It's people *in* the middle classes that disgust me.'

'Can middle-class people be from the middle class in your sense?'

'Oh, yes,' said Nicholas generously, 'Victor is an outstanding case.'

Victor smiled to show that he was enjoying himself.

'It's easier for girls, of course,' Nicholas continued. 'Marriage is such a blessing, hoisting women from dreary backgrounds into a wider world.' He glanced at Bridget. 'All a chap can really do, unless he's the sort of queer who spends his whole time writing postcards to people who might need a spare man, is to toe the line. And be thoroughly charming and well informed,' he added, with a reassuring smile for Victor.

'Nicholas, of course, is an expert,' David intervened, 'having personally raised several women from the gutter.'

'At considerable expense,' Nicholas agreed.

'The cost of being dragged into the gutter was even higher, wouldn't you say, Nicholas?' said David, reminding Nicholas of his political humiliation. 'Either way, the gutter seems to be where you feel at home.'

'Cor blimey, guv,' said Nicholas in his comical cockney voice. 'When you've gorn down the drain like wot I 'ave, the gutter looks like a bed o' roses.'

Eleanor still found it inexplicable that the best English manners contained such a high proportion of outright rudeness and gladiatorial combat. She knew that David abused this licence, but she also knew how 'boring' it was to interfere with the exercise of unkindness. When David reminded someone of their weaknesses and failures she was torn between a desire to save the victim, whose feelings she adopted as her own, and an equally strong desire not to be accused of spoiling a game. The more she thought about this conflict, the more tightly it trapped her. She would never know what to say because whatever she said would be wrong.

Eleanor thought about her stepfather barking at her mother across the wastes of English silver, French furniture, and Chinese vases that helped to prevent him from becoming physically violent. This dwarfish and impotent French duke had dedicated his life to the idea that civilization had died in 1789. He nonetheless accepted a ten per cent cut from the dealers who sold pre-revolutionary antiques to his wife. He had forced Mary to sell her mother's Monets and Bonnards on the ground that they were examples of a decadent art that would never really matter. To him, Mary was the least valuable object in the fastidious museums they inhabited, and when eventually he bullied her to death he felt that he had eliminated the last trace of modernity from his life except, of course, for the enormous income that now came to him from the sales of a dry-cleaning fluid made in Ohio.

Eleanor had watched her mother's persecution with the same vivid silence as she experienced in the face of her own gradual disintegration tonight. Although she was not a cruel person, she remembered being helpless with laughter watching her stepfather, by then suffering from Parkinson's disease, lift a forkful of peas, only to find the fork empty by the time it reached his mouth. Yet she had never told him how much she hated him. She had not spoken then, and she would not speak now.

'Look at Eleanor,' said David, 'she has that expression she only puts on when she is thinking of her dear rich dead mother. I'm right, aren't I, darling?' he cajoled her. 'Aren't I?'

'Yes, you are,' she admitted.

'Eleanor's mother and aunt,' said David in the tone of a man reading *Little Red Riding Hood* to a gullible child, 'thought that they could buy human antiques. The moth-eaten bearers of ancient titles were reupholstered with thick wads of dollars, but,' he concluded with a warm banality which could not altogether conceal his humorous intentions, 'you just can't treat human beings like things.'

'Definitely,' said Bridget, amazed to hear herself speak.

'You agree with me?' said David, suddenly attentive.

'Definitely,' said Bridget, who appeared to have broken her silence on somewhat limited terms.

'Maybe the human antiques wanted to be bought,' Anne suggested.

'Nobody doubts that,' said David, 'I'm sure they were licking the windowpane. What's so shocking is that after being saved, they dared to rear up on their spindly Louis Quinze legs and start giving orders. The *ingratitude*!'

'Cor!' said Nicholas. 'Wot I wouldn't give for some o' 'em Looey Can's legs – they must be wurf a bob or two.'

Victor was embarrassed on Eleanor's behalf. After all, she was paying for dinner.

Bridget was confused by David. She agreed whole-heartedly with what he had said about people not being things. In fact, once she'd been tripping and had realized with overwhelming clarity that what was wrong with the world was people treating each other like things. It was such a big idea that it was hard to hold on to, but she had felt very strongly about it at the time, and she thought David was trying to say the same thing. She also admired him for being the only person who frightened Nicholas. On the other hand, she could see why he frightened Nicholas.

Anne had had enough. She felt a combination of boredom and rebelliousness which reminded her of adolescence. She could take no more of David's mood, and the way he baited Eleanor, tormented Nicholas, silenced Bridget, and even diminished Victor.

'Sorry,' she murmured to Eleanor, 'I'll be right back.'

In the dim hallway, she pulled a cigarette out of her bag and lit it. The flaming match was reflected in all the mirrors around the hall, and made a sliver of glass shine momentarily at the foot of the stairs. Stooping down to pick up the glass with the tip of her index finger, Anne suddenly knew that she was being watched and, looking up, she saw Patrick sitting on the widest step where the staircase curved. He wore flannel pyjamas with blue elephants on them, but his face looked downcast.

'Hi, Patrick,' said Anne, 'you look so grim. Can't you get to sleep?'

He did not answer or move. 'I just have to get rid of this piece of glass,' said Anne. 'I guess something broke here earlier?'

'It was me,' said Patrick.

'Hang on one second,' she said.

She's lying, thought Patrick, she won't come back.

There was no wastepaper basket in the hall, but she brushed the glass off her finger into a porcelain umbrella stand that bristled with David's collection of exotic canes.

She hurried back to Patrick and sat on the step beneath him. 'Did you cut yourself on that glass?' she asked tenderly, putting her hand on his arm.

He pulled away from her and said, 'Leave me alone.'

'Do you want me to get your mother?' asked Anne.

'All right,' said Patrick.

'OK. I'll go get her right away,' said Anne. Back in the dining room, she heard Nicholas saying to Victor, 'David and I were meaning to ask you before dinner whether John Locke really said that a man who forgot his crimes should not be punished for them.'

'Yes, indeed,' said Victor. 'He maintained that personal identity depended on continuity of memory. In the case of a forgotten crime one would be punishing the wrong person.'

'I'll drink to that,' said Nicholas.

Anne leaned over to Eleanor and said to her quietly, 'I think you ought to go and see Patrick. He was sitting on the stairs asking for you.'

'Thank you,' whispered Eleanor.

'Perhaps it should be the other way round,' said David. 'A man who remembers his crimes can usually be relied upon to punish himself, whereas the law should punish the person who is irresponsible enough to forget.'

'D'you believe in capital punishment?' piped up Bridget.

'Not since it ceased to be a public occasion,' said

David. 'In the eighteenth century a hanging was a really good day's outing.'

'Everybody enjoyed themselves: even the man who was being hanged,' added Nicholas.

'Fun for all the family,' David went on. 'Isn't that the phrase everybody uses nowadays? God knows, it's always what *I* aim for, but an occasional trip to Tyburn must have made the task easier.'

Nicholas giggled. Bridget wondered what Tyburn was. Eleanor smiled feebly, and pushed her chair back.

'Not leaving us I hope, darling,' said David.

'I have to . . . I'll be back in a moment,' Eleanor mumbled.

'I didn't quite catch that: you have to be back in a moment?'

'There's something I have to do.'

'Well, hurry, hurry, hurry,' said David gallantly, 'we'll be lost without your conversation.'

Eleanor walked to the door at the same time as Yvette opened it carrying a silver coffee pot.

'I found Patrick on the stairs,' Anne said. 'He seemed kind of sad.'

David's eyes darted towards Eleanor's back as she slipped past Yvette. 'Darling,' he said, and then more peremptorily, 'Eleanor.'

She turned, her teeth locked onto a thumbnail, trying to get a grip that would hold. She often tore at the stunted nails when she was not smoking. 'Yes?' she said.

'I thought that we'd agreed that you wouldn't rush to Patrick each time he whines and blubbers.'

'But he fell down earlier and he may have hurt himself.'

'In that case,' said David with sudden seriousness, 'he may need a doctor.' He rested the palms of his hands on the top of the table, as if to rise.

'Oh, I don't think he's hurt,' said Anne, to restrain David. She had a strong feeling that she would not be keeping her promise to Patrick if she sent him his father rather than his mother. 'He just wants to be comforted.'

'You see, darling,' said David, 'he isn't hurt, and so it is just a sentimental question: does one indulge the self-pity of a child, or not? Does one allow oneself to be blackmailed, or not? Come and sit down – we can at least discuss it.'

Eleanor edged her way back to her chair reluctantly. She knew she would be pinned down by a conversation that would defeat her, but not persuade her.

'The proposition I want to make,' said David, 'is that education should be something of which a child can later say: if I survived that, I can survive anything.'

'That's crazy and wrong,' said Anne, 'and you know it.'

'I certainly think that children should be stretched to the limit of their abilities,' said Victor, 'but I'm equally certain they can't be if they're intensely miserable.'

'Nobody wants to make anybody miserable,' said Nicholas, puffing out his cheeks incredulously. 'We're just saying that it doesn't do the child any good to be molly-coddled. I may be a frightful reactionary, but I think that all you have to do for children is hire a reasonable nanny and put them down for Eton.'

'What, the nannies?' said Bridget giggling. 'Anyway, what if you have a girl?'

Nicholas looked at her sternly.

'I guess that putting things down is your speciality,' said Anne to Nicholas.

'Oh, I know it's an unfashionable view to hold these days,' Nicholas went on complacently, 'but in my opinion nothing that happens to you as a child really matters.'

'If we're getting down to things that don't really matter,' said Anne, 'you're top of my list.'

'Oh, my word,' said Nicholas, in his sports commentator's voice, 'a ferocious backhand from the young American woman, but the line judge rules it out.'

'From what you've told me,' said Bridget, still elated by the thought of nannies in tailcoats, 'nothing much that happened in *your* childhood did matter: you just did what everyone expected.' Feeling a vague pressure on her right thigh, she glanced round at David, but he seemed to be staring ahead, organizing a sceptical expression on his face. The pressure stopped. On her other side, Victor peeled a nectarine with hurried precision.

'It's true,' said Nicholas, making a visible effort at equanimity, 'that my childhood was uneventful. People never remember happiness with the care that they lavish on preserving every detail of their suffering. I remember stroking my cheek against the velvet collar of my overcoat. Asking my grandfather for pennies to throw into that golden pool at the Ritz. Big lawns. Buckets and spades. That sort of thing.'

Bridget could not concentrate on what Nicholas was saying. She felt cold metal against her knee. Looking down, she saw David lifting the edge of her dress with a small silver knife and running it along her thigh. What the fuck did he think he was doing? She frowned at him reproachfully. He merely pressed the point a little more firmly into her thigh, without looking at her.

Victor wiped the tips of his fingers with his napkin,

while answering a question which Bridget had missed. He sounded a little bored and not surprisingly, when she heard what he had to say. 'Certainly if the degree of psychological connectedness and psychological continuity have become sufficiently weakened, it would be true to say that a person should look upon his childhood with no more than charitable curiosity.'

Bridget's mind flashed back to her father's foolish conjuring tricks, and her mother's ghastly floral-print dresses, but charitable curiosity was not what she felt.

'Would you like one of these?' said David, lifting a fig from the bowl in the middle of the table. 'They're at their best at this time of year.'

'No, thanks,' she said.

David pinched the fig firmly between his fingers and pushed it towards Bridget's mouth, 'Come on,' he said, 'I know how much you like them.'

Bridget opened her mouth obediently and took the fig between her teeth. She blushed because the table had fallen silent and she knew that everyone was watching her. As soon as she could she took the fig from her mouth and asked David if she could borrow his knife to peel it with. David admired her for the speed and stealth of this tactic and handed over the knife.

Eleanor watched Bridget take the fig with a familiar

sense of doom. She could never see David impose his will on anyone without considering how often he had imposed it on her.

At the root of her dread was the fragmented memory of the night when Patrick was conceived. Against her will, she pictured the Cornish house on its narrow headland, always damp, always grey, more Atlantic than earth. He had pushed the hollow base of her skull against the corner of the marble table. When she had broken free he had punched the back of her knees and made her fall on the stairs and raped her there, with her arms twisted back. She had hated him like a stranger and hated him like a traitor. God, how she had loathed him, but when she had become pregnant she had said she would stay if he never, *never* touched her again.

Bridget chewed the fig unenthusiastically. As Anne watched her, she could not help thinking of the age-old question which every woman asks herself at some time or other: do I have to swallow it? She wondered whether to picture Bridget as a collared slave draped over the feet of an oriental bully, or as a rebellious schoolgirl being forced to eat the apple pie she tried to leave behind at lunch. She suddenly felt quite detached from the company around her.

Nicholas struck Anne as more pathetic than he had

before. He was just one of those Englishmen who was always saying silly things to sound less pompous, and pompous things to sound less silly. They turned into self-parodies without going to the trouble of acquiring a self first. David, who thought he was the Creature from the Black Lagoon, was just a higher species of this involuted failure. She looked at Victor slumped round-shouldered over the remains of his nectarine. He had not kept up the half-clever banter which he usually felt it his duty to provide. She could remember him earlier in the summer saying, 'I may spend my days doubting doubting, but when it comes to gossip I like *hard* facts.' From then on it had been nothing but hard facts. Today he was different. Perhaps he really wanted to do some work again.

Eleanor's crushed expression no longer moved her either. The only thing that made Anne's detachment falter was the thought of Patrick waiting on the stairs, his disappointment widening as he waited, but it only spurred her on to the same conclusion: that she wanted nothing more to do with these people, that it was time to leave, even if Victor would be embarrassed by leaving early. She looked over to Victor, raising her eyebrows and darting her eyes towards the door. Instead of the little frown she had expected from him, Victor nodded his head discreetly as if agreeing with the pepper mill. Anne let a few moments go by then leaned over to Eleanor and said, 'It's sad, but I think we really must leave. It's been a long day, you must be tired too.'

'Yes,' said Victor firmly, 'I must get up early tomorrow morning and make some progress with my work.' He heaved himself up and started to thank Eleanor and David before they had time to organize the usual protests.

In fact, David hardly looked up. He continued to run his thumbnail around the sealed end of his cigar, 'You know the way out,' he said, in response to their thanks, 'I hope you'll forgive me for not coming to wave goodbye.'

'Never,' said Anne, more seriously than she had intended.

Eleanor knew there was a formula everybody used in these situations, but she searched for it in vain. Whenever she thought of what she was meant to say, it seemed to dash around the corner, and lose itself in the crowd of things she should not say. The most successful fugitives were often the dullest, the sentences that nobody notices until they are not spoken: 'How nice to see you . . . won't you stay a little longer . . . what a good idea . . .'

Victor closed the dining room door behind him carefully, like a man who does not want to wake a sleeping sentry. He smiled at Anne and she smiled back, and they were suddenly conscious of how relieved they were to be leaving the Melroses. They started to laugh silently and to tiptoe towards the hall.

'I'll just check if Patrick is still here,' Anne whispered.

'Why are we whispering?' Victor whispered.

'I don't know,' Anne whispered back. She looked up the staircase. It was empty. He had obviously grown tired of waiting and gone back to bed. 'I guess he's asleep,' she said to Victor.

They went out of the front door and up the wide steps towards their car. The moon was bruised by thin cloud and surrounded by a ring of dispersed light.

'You can't say I didn't try,' said Anne, 'I was hanging right in there until Nicholas and David started outlining their educational programme. If some big-deal friend of theirs, like George, was feeling sad and lonely they would fly back to England and *personally* mix the dry martinis and load the shotguns, but when David's own son is feeling sad and lonely in the room next door, they fight every attempt to make him less miserable.'

'You're right,' said Victor, opening the car door, 'in the end one must oppose cruelty, at the very least by refusing to take part in it.'

'Underneath that New and Lingwood shirt,' said Anne, 'beats a heart of gold.'

Must you leave so soon? thought Eleanor. *That* was the phrase. She had remembered it. Better late than never was another phrase, not really true in this case. Sometimes things were too late, too late the very moment they happened. Other people knew what they were meant to say, knew what they were meant to mean, and other people still – otherer people – knew what the other people meant when they said it. God, she was drunk. When her eyes watered, the candle flames looked like a liqueur advertisement, splintering into mahogany-coloured spines of light. Not drunk enough to stop the half-thoughts from sputtering on into the night, keeping her from any rest. Maybe she could go to Patrick now. Whatshername had slipped off cunningly just after Victor and Anne left. Maybe they would let her go too. But what if they didn't? She could not stand another failure, she could not bow down another time. And so she did nothing for a little longer.

'If nothing matters, you're top of my list,' Nicholas

quoted, with a little yelp of delight. 'One has to admire Victor, who tries so hard to be conventional, for never having an entirely conventional girlfriend.'

'Almost nothing is as entertaining as the contortions of a clever Jewish snob,' said David.

'Very broad-minded of you to have him in your house,' said Nicholas, in his judge's voice. 'Some members of the jury may feel that it is *too* broad-minded, but that is not for me to say,' he boomed, adjusting an imaginary wig. 'The openness of English society has always been its great strength: the entrepreneurs and arrivistes of yesterday – the Cecils, for example – become the guardians of stability in a mere three or four hundred years. Nevertheless, there is no principle, however laudable in itself, which cannot be perverted. Whether the openness and the generosity of what the press chooses to call "the establishment" has been abused on this occasion, by welcoming into its midst a dangerous intellectual of murky Semitic origins is for you, and for you alone, to judge.'

David grinned. He was in the mood for fun. After all, what redeemed life from complete horror was the almost unlimited number of things to be nasty about. All he needed now was to ditch Eleanor, who was twitching silently like a beetle on its back, get a bottle of brandy, and settle down to gossip with Nicholas. It was too perfect. 'Let's go into the drawing room,' he said.

'Fine,' said Nicholas, who knew that he had won David over and did not want to lose this privilege by paying any attention to Eleanor. He got up, drained his glass of wine, and followed David to the drawing room.

Eleanor remained frozen in her chair, unable to believe how lucky she was to be completely alone. Her mind rushed ahead to a tender reconciliation with Patrick, but she stayed slumped in front of the debris of dinner. The door opened and Eleanor jumped. It was only Yvette.

'*Oh, pardon, Madame, je ne savais pas que vous étiez toujours là.*'

'*Non, non, je vais justement partir,*' said Eleanor apologetically. She went through the kitchen and up the back stairs to avoid Nicholas and David, walking the whole length of the corridor to see whether Patrick was still waiting for her on the staircase. He was not there. Instead of being grateful that he had already gone to bed, she felt even more guilty that she had not come to console him earlier.

She opened the door to his room gently, excruciated by the whining of the hinge. Patrick was asleep in his bed. Rather than disturb him, she tiptoed back out of the room.

Patrick lay awake. His heart was pounding. He knew it was his mother, but she had come too late. He would not call to her again. When he had still been waiting on the stairs and the door of the hall opened, he stayed to see if it was his mother, and he hid in case it was his father. But it was only that woman who had lied to him. Everybody used his name but they did not know who he was. One day he would play football with the heads of his enemies.

Who the fuck did he think he was? How dare he poke a knife up her dress? Bridget pictured herself strangling David as he sat in his dining-room chair, her thumbs pressing into his windpipe. And then, confusingly, she imagined that she had fallen into his lap, while she was strangling him, and she could feel that he had a huge erection. 'Gross out,' she said aloud, 'totally gross.' At least David was intense, intensely gross, but intense. Unlike Nicholas, who turned out to be a complete cringer, really pathetic. And the others were so boring. How was she meant to spend another second in this house?

Bridget wanted a joint to take the edge off her

indignation. She opened her suitcase and took a plastic bag out of the toe of her back-up pair of cowboy boots. The bag contained some dark green grass that she had already taken the seeds and stalks out of, and a packet of orange Rizlas. She sat down at an amusing Gothic desk fitted between the bedroom's two round windows. Sheaves of engraved writing paper were housed under its tallest arch, with envelopes in the smaller arches either side. On the desk's open flap was a black leather pad holding a large piece of blotting paper. She rolled a small joint above it and then brushed the escaped leaves carefully back into her bag.

Turning off the light to create a more ceremonial and private atmosphere, Bridget sat down in the curved windowsill and lit her joint. The moon had risen above the thin clouds and cast deep shadows on the terrace. She sucked a thick curl of smoke appreciatively into her lungs and held it in, noticing how the dull glow of the fig leaves made them look as if they were cut out of old pewter. As she blew the smoke slowly through the little holes in the mosquito net she heard the door open beneath her window.

'Why are blazers so common?' she heard Nicholas ask.

'Because they're worn by ghastly people like him,'

David answered.

God, didn't they ever grow tired of bitching about people? thought Bridget. Or, at least, about people she didn't know. Or did she know him? With a little flash of shame and paranoia Bridget remembered that her father wore blazers. Perhaps they were trying to humiliate her. She held her breath and sat absolutely still. She could see them now, both smoking their cigars. They started to walk down the terrace, their conversation fading as they headed towards the far end. She took another toke on her joint; it had almost gone out, but she got it going again. The bastards were probably talking about her, but she might just be thinking that because she was stoned. Well, she *was* stoned and she did think that. Bridget smiled. She wished she had someone to be silly with. Licking her finger she doused down the side of the joint that was burning too fast. They were pacing back now and she could hear again what they were saying.

'I suppose I would have to answer that,' Nicholas said, 'with the remark that Croyden made – not quoted, incidentally, in his memorial service – when he was found emerging from a notorious public lavatory in Hackney.' Nicholas's voice rose an octave, ' "I have pursued beauty wherever it has led me, even to the most unbeautiful places."'

'Not a bad policy,' said David, 'if a little fruitily expressed.'

12

When they got back home, Anne was in a good mood. She flopped down on the brown sofa, kicked off her shoes, and lit a cigarette. 'Everybody knows you've got a great mind,' she said to Victor, 'but what interests me is your slightly less well-known body.'

Victor laughed a little nervously and walked across the room to pour himself a glass of whisky. 'Reputation isn't everything,' he said.

'Come over here,' Anne ordered softly.

'Drink?' asked Victor.

Anne shook her head. She watched Victor drop a couple of ice cubes into his glass.

He walked over to the sofa and sat down beside her, smiling benignly.

When she leaned forward to kiss him, he fished one

of the ice cubes out of the glass and, with unexpected swiftness, slipped it down the front of her dress.

'Oh, God,' gasped Anne, trying to keep her composure, 'that's deliciously cool and refreshing. And wet,' she added, wriggling and pushing the ice cube further down under her black dress.

Victor put his hand under her dress and retrieved the ice cube expertly, putting it in his mouth and sucking it before letting it slip from his mouth back into the glass. 'I thought you needed cooling off,' he said, putting his palms firmly on each of her knees.

'Oh, my,' Anne purred, in a southern drawl, 'despite outward appearances, I can see you're a man of strong appetites.' She lifted one of her feet onto the sofa and reached out her hand at the same time to run her fingers through the thick waves of Victor's hair. She pulled his head gently towards the stretched tendon of her raised thigh. Victor kissed the white cotton of her underwear and grazed it like a man catching a grape between his teeth.

Unable to sleep, Eleanor put on a Japanese dressing gown and retreated to her car. She felt strangely elated in the white leather interior of the Buick, with her packet of Player's and the bottle of cognac she retrieved from under the driving seat. Her happiness was complete when she turned on Radio Monte Carlo and found that it was playing one of her favourite songs: 'I Got Plenty o' Nuttin'' from *Porgy and Bess*. She mouthed the words silently, 'And nuttin's plenty for me,' dipping her head from side to side, almost in time with the music.

When she saw Bridget hobbling along in the moonlight with a suitcase banging against her knee, Eleanor thought, not for the first time, that she must be hallucinating. What on earth was the girl doing? Well, it was really very obvious. She was leaving. The simplicity of the act horrified Eleanor. After years of dreaming about how to tunnel under the guardroom undetected, she was amazed to see a newcomer walk out through the open gate. Just going down the drive as if she were free.

Bridget swung her suitcase from one hand to another. She wasn't sure it would fit on the back of Barry's bike. The whole thing was a total freakout. She had left Nicholas in bed, snoring as usual, like an old pig with terminal flu. The idea was to dump her suitcase at the bottom of the drive and go back to fetch it once she had met up with Barry. She swapped hands again. The lure of the Open Road definitely lost some of its appeal if you took any luggage with you.

Two-thirty by the village church, that's what Barry had said on the phone before dinner. She dropped her suitcase into a clump of rosemary, letting out a petulant sigh to show herself she was more irritated than frightened. What if the village didn't have a church? What if her suitcase was stolen? How far was it to the village anyway? God, life was so complicated. She had run away from home once when she was nine, but doubled back because she couldn't bear to think what her parents might say while she was away.

As she joined the small road that led down to the village, Bridget found herself walled in by pines. The shadows thickened until the moonlight no longer shone on the road. A light wind animated the branches of the tall trees. Full of dread, Bridget suddenly came to a stop. Was Barry really a fun person when it came down to it? After making their appointment he had said, 'Be there or be square!' At the time she was so infatuated by the idea of escaping Nicholas and the Melroses that she had forgotten to be annoyed, but now she realized just how annoying it was.

Eleanor was wondering whether to get another bottle of cognac (cognac was for the car because it was so stimulating), or go back to bed and drink whisky. Either way she had to return to the house. When she was about to open the car door she saw Bridget again. This time she was staggering up the drive, dragging her suitcase. Eleanor felt cool and detached. She decided that nothing could surprise her any longer. Perhaps Bridget did this every evening for the exercise. Or maybe she wanted a lift somewhere. Eleanor preferred to watch her than to get involved, so long as Bridget got back into the house quickly.

Bridget thought she heard the sound of a radio, but she lost it again amid the rustle of leaves. She was shaken and rather embarrassed by her escapade. Plus her arms were about to drop off. Well, never mind, at least she had asserted herself, sort of. She opened the door of the house. It squeaked. Luckily, she could rely on Nicholas to be sleeping like a drugged elephant, so that no sound could possibly reach him. But what if she woke David? *Freak-ee*. Another squeak and she closed the door behind her. As she crept down the corridor she could hear a sort of moaning and then a yelping shout, like a cry of pain.

David woke up with a shout of fear. Why the hell did people say, 'It's *only* a dream'? His dreams exhausted and dismembered him. They seemed to open onto a deeper layer of insomnia, as if he was only lulled to sleep in order to be shown that he could not rest. Tonight he had dreamed that he was the cripple in Athens airport. He could feel his limbs twisted like vine stumps, his wobbling head burrowing this way and that as he tried to throw himself forward, and his unfriendly hands slapping his own face. In the waiting room at the airport all the passengers were people he knew: the barman from the Central in Lacoste, George, Bridget, people from decades of London parties, all talking and reading books. And there he was, heaving himself across the room one leg dragging behind him, trying to say, 'Hello, it's David Melrose, I hope you aren't deceived by this absurd disguise,' but he only managed to moan, or as he grew more desperate, to squeal, while he tossed advertisements for roasted nuts at them with upsetting inaccuracy. He could see the embarrassment in some of their faces, and feigned blankness in others. And he heard George say to his neighbour, 'What a perfectly ghastly man.'

David turned on the light and fumbled for his copy of *Jorrocks Rides Again*. He wondered whether Patrick would remember. There was always repression, of course, although it didn't seem to work very well on his own desires. He must *try* not to do it again, that really would be tempting fate. David could not help smiling at his own audacity.

Patrick did not wake up from his dream, although he could feel a needle slip under his shoulder blade and push out through his chest. The thick thread was sewing his lungs up like an old sack until he could not breathe. Panic like wasps hovering about his face, ducking and twisting and beating the air.

He saw the Alsatian that had chased him in the woods, and he felt he was running through the rattling yellow leaves again with wider and wider strides. As the dog drew closer and was about to get him, Patrick started adding up numbers out loud, and at the last moment his body lifted off the ground until he was looking down on the tops of the trees, as if at seaweed over the side of a boat. He knew that he must never allow himself to fall asleep. Below him the Alsatian scrambled to a halt in a flurry of dry leaves and picked up a dead branch in its mouth.

picador.com

blog
videos
interviews
extracts